CAUGHT UP BETWEEN A BOSS AND A THUG

DANIELLE NORRINGTON

Caught Up Between A Boss and A Thug
Copyright © 2019 by Danielle Norrington
Published by Shan Presents
www.shanpresents.com

Subscribe

Text Shan to 22828 to stay up to date with new releases, sneak peeks, contest, and more....

Submissions

To submit your manuscript to Shan Presents, please send
the first three chapters and synopsis to
submissions@shanpresents.com

Chapter 1

The sun hadn't even risen in the sky yet. Birds and people alike were still asleep. After checking her makeup making sure everything is covered, Deja heads out the door, her eyes glancing at the couch to see was her son on it or not. She hadn't heard a phone call from him or anything. I guess as long as she doesn't hear about him on the news or Facebook, he's okay.

Deja kept moving, exiting her apartment and locking it behind her. It's a good thing Big Doug didn't mess with her car.

Like always, she made it to work on time. With Deja and another woman being the only two in the restaurant, she went straight into preparing the coffee and pastries while the other woman did the easiest shit. Her coworker likes wiping down tables that's already cleaned and doing the inventory from last night.

Minutes before their first customer walks in, Deja receives a text from Raine off Facebook messenger saying that Marterrio just made it through the door, and he's packing his things.

1

Everyone has that one coworker that doesn't want to do nothing but ride the clock and make easy money. With Deja son trying to leave after being gone for nearly a whole day and she and her girls about to be homeless, Deja couldn't deal with this shit from her coworker.

"Thank you sweetie," the White elderly woman says after paying for her hot cup of coffee and two cheese danishes; she then smiles. Deja was ready to walk away from the counter but the woman remains. "Can you walk me to my car dear?" she asks Deja with a smile. Her brows pressed together, confused and unsure.

"I'm not sure if that's okay to do," Deja says instead. Of course she's seen the old woman come in a few times and get the same order, but she didn't trust herself being along with an old White woman; she could be a low key supremacist. Her grandson could be a harvester of organs for all Deja knew! Who knows? She didn't want to find out.

"You know, everyday I'm there for my son before we wake up and heads out to work. I make sure he had his favorite coffee and sweet delights in the morning to help him have a good day at work," she smiles at Deja.

"That's good and all, but I have to get going. Every day I come to this job and I do it well, and I fight for my family. Like now. Excuse me," she says and then finally rushes away from the cash register. Deja didn't bother clocking out or telling her other coworker her whereabouts. She snatches off her apron and then got to her car so fast.

Deja made it from her first job and back to her apartment quicker than before, running two red lights and catching road rage along the way. Leaving her car running, pacing herself, Deja went up the flight of stairs by twos until she reached the corridor that led down to her apartment.

Right as she opens the door, there was Marterrio on his way out with two of her black garbage bags in both hands.

"Son, I haven't seen you all yesterday. Where are you going?" she asks him, pulling Marterrio back inside.

Marterrio gently shakes his head, "Ma, I can't do this with you anymore. You got this Big Doug nigga laying up on you and stuff."

"That's over with, baby. Me and him are done now. Come and sit down, and talk to me. Why do you have your bags packed? Where are you going?"

Obedient and patient, Marterrio walks away from the front door with his mother and they have a seat on the couch.

"My girl Denise offered me her place to stay at," he says. "I'm going to live with her."

Deja bit her tongue. Her son had brains, and he has a high school diploma. He's intelligent, but he loves the streets just as much as Deja and Jayceon did. He won't settle down for Denise and she won't understand that she can't have him all to herself.

"Are you sure that's what you really want?" Deja calmly asks her son. "Cause I want you to think this over. You see a person for how they really is when you move in with them."

"I'm sure mom. I'm a man now and I have to get out here on my own. Here," he reaches into his pocket. Deja watches as he pulls a wad of cash out from it and then hands it to her.

"Baby, where did you get this?" she asks him.

"Don't worry about it. I know you need it. I'll hustle on some more when I get the chance."

"Son that's not living," Deja shakes her head. She didn't want to accept the cash, but they didn't have long to move and she didn't get paid until next week.

3

"Seeing you work two jobs and still struggling ain't it neither momma."

"You think that's struggling? We're about to be put out in four more days, Marterrio. So, I've learned my lesson with him. But I want you to make sure that this is what you really want."

"You can use the money to pay the rent right?"

"It's not enough, Marterrio," Deja firmly glances at him. Raine loudly sighs on the side of them as Marterrio was now speechless.

Sitting beside his mom with his things packed in garbage bags to go and live with a female that's well off without him, Marterrio had to decide. Go live with Denise and have her trying to control him or stick things out with his mom, the leading lady of his life. His little sisters needs him.

"What can I do to help mom?" Marterrio says after rubbing his hands over his head.

"You're here to stay?" Deja asks him.

"Yea, what type of son would I be to leave you and my sisters?"

"I'm going to take this money and get us a motel room somewhere. What you can do is work on getting your license so you can drive my car and find you somewhere to work. I have to get back to work," Deja gets up from sitting down and then exits the apartment.

Deja returns back to work with no problem and continues her shift. For some apparent reason, she had expected that Big Doug would call the police on her and get her locked up for banging him up, but Deja remembered he lived by a code; no snitching. She had lumps and bruises on her too. There's no other way Big Doug could break Deja down like he did when he let her rent get behind. He should've known that was going to be his ass.

4

Part time server by day and janitor by night, Deja didn't have time to cook dinner during the weekdays nor pack their things. Five days a week, she leaves one job, come home and takes a two hour nap and then leave out the door to another one.

Deja favors her night time job more. It's enough money, and she works alone with no supervision plus she's able to grab and hide little small things for her house. Both jobs were paying the bills and kept Deja and her family afloat until Douglas came into the picture.

Them staying at a motel room lasted longer than Deja imagined for it to be. She didn't expect their stay there to extend past two weeks but with her background, finding a landlord to accept her is hard.

Rylee didn't understand why she wasn't eating home cooked meals or have all her toys, but she didn't complain at all. It broke Deja to see the silent and confused look on Rylee's face, but she didn't fold. With the help of Marterrio, he and Deja did the best they could.

With their sub-sandwiches made from an Asian cook, Deja and her kids were on their way back to the motel when they see an ambulance on the lot. Raine hates it here. Someone was always arguing and beating on that person's door. There's a sprung out junkie with a scratch or a prostitute in tiny clothes. Then you had the drug dealers next door; sometimes you could smell the dope so loud coming through the thin walls. At night time, the Montico Inn came alive with its tenants.

"I've been thinking of working at Chick-Fil-A, mom," Raine says.

"Have you reached out to your dad?" Deja asks from the driver's seat, her eyes fixed on the road.

"No," Raine says in a low voice.

"Then try him first," Deja says, stopping at a red light.

5

She quickly did something she hasn't did in a long time, retrieving a cigarette and then lightening it.

"Mommy, when will we see daddy?" Rylee inquires.

"I don't know baby, probably for the holidays."

"What's the holidays?" Rylee later asks. Deja deeply exhales the cigarette smoke, cracking the window on her side. She doesn't reply to Rylee and continues driving.

Deja preferred for all of them to get out of the car at once and go up to their room together, but sometimes she couldn't stop Raine from going back to the car for always forgetting something. Being the mother she is with her instinct that Raine was being a hot ass teenager, Deja lingers behind and follows after Raine.

Moving fast, Raine made her way down the corridor and then descends the stairs. "Hey girl," her boyfriend, Tyriq grabs her from out of nowhere as soon as she reaches the ground. Raine giggles and they quickly exchange a kiss on the lips.

"Hey," she sings, happy to see him. "I miss you," she says, pulling away from him.

"Y'all still here. Your mom can't get right can she?"

"Don't talk about my mom. She's doing the best she can right now."

"Yeah, well I can show you how to get some real money, baby girl."

"Yea?" she was intrigued. Raine would do anything to help her mom.

"Hell yes. Men will pay hundreds of dollars just for you to show up on dates with them or whatever," he says. It sounds convincing to her.

"But ain't that's like selling pussy?"

"Hell no!" Tyriq denies and then pulls her in closer. "I gotta fellow right now with at least two hundred on him.

All they be wanting you to do is look pretty and rub on their leg here and there. You down?" Tyriq holds her gaze in his eyes, his hand racing down to her backside and then to her butt. He grabs a handful of her cheek in his hand and then squeezes it before releasing.

"Yea," Raine says in a low voice, too mesmerized by his deep brown eyes to understand what she was saying. Her mind didn't register the meaning of his words; she just knew she wants to help.

"Oh no the fuck she isn't!" her mom says from around the corner. They didn't see her coming or Marterrio. Both of them had emerged from the darkness like thieves in an alley.

"Mom!" Raine exclaims after being pushed out of the way. Deja is strong and still good at street fighting for her age. Seeing them punch Tyriq in the stomach a couple of times with his back against the brick wall, she cuffs her mouth. Raine never seen her mom in action before until now. Most times, her mom fought guys behind a closed door.

"You stay away from my daughter, boy! Or next time your little ass gone end up dead somewhere in a back alley. The police won't be able to identify you! Get your ass out of here," Deja hollers at him, her blood pumping through her veins. Marterrio releases Tyriq and they all watch as he scatters away, hoping that he'd hop in a car but he climbed onto a bike and was out of there.

"Mom -" Raine says, abruptly cut off from Deja. She raises her hand and slaps Raine hard.

"Girl is you stupid or something? Do you have any idea that that nigga was finna put you on a hoe track?"

"A what?" Raine holds the side of her face, and with tears in her eyes.

7

"I said a hoe track!" Deja repeats. "And sucking one dick won't get you a easy two hundred dollars neither, Raine. Get your ass to the room now!" Deja orders her.

Deja didn't care to give it much thought of whether she was too hard on Raine or not! Running tricks is something that Deja never saw herself doing and neither will her daughter. Hoeing isn't easy to break as thieving is. If you're real pretty, a pimp will hound you and control you.

The following day was an off day, and Deja's third rejection on her application for an apartment. Something just have to give. She hated the fact her son was out here hustling and selling dope and now her daughter wants to sell her body. Her checks were becoming smaller and smaller because of the fact that she took shorter hours to keep eyes on Raine more. *This ain't living!*

Deja has been irritated all day long, starting with her first job and then getting off to Raine and Marterrio bumping heads. Now at work on her second job, Deja had the music turned loud on her phone as she now enters the financial secretary office. Something was telling her that there isn't a miracle in this room, but her mind knew better.

Carefully listening to see if anyone of her coworkers were approaching, Deja closes the door halfway as if she's handling the trash, blocking the view of the camera into the room. She swiftly moves around the desk and then pulls at the middle locked drawer. Deja searched and checked the rest of the drawers for something sharp she could use. She had to see!

Taking the spare bobbin pin from her hair and a stick pin, Deja worked diligently and fast, unlocking the drawer lock. She then goes back behind the door and swiftly changes the trash, opening the door wider again. Deja's heart was beating so fast and loud, she could hear it more than her music.

It was now time to clean the desk area, and that's when Deja was able to open the drawer wide enough, seeing the cash as she guessed. *Stupid secretary!* The woman had stashed away at least two hundred thousand dollars.

It's wrong to steal and it's not like Deja needed the cash, but a better motel than the one they were at would've been just fine. She couldn't steal from her job that helps her stay afloat. Deja passed on the money and continues her work, later crying in the restroom stall when she found a moment alone.

She could've went straight back to the motel and be with her kids, but Deja had an urge she couldn't get rid of and that was for her to land her hands on some money. She has to! With her half tank of gas in the car, she took the time out and scoped out abandoned houses and even the rich folks' neighborhood. Seeing a young white couple walking and holding hands, Deja went for an opportunity the moment she saw it, knowing that she had no other choice.

"The fuck is they doing walking this late at night anyway? They're so fucking safe in their neighborhood, huh?" she suckles her teeth and then reaches in the backseat and gets her long black wig and plastic mask. *Gotdamn, happy and wealthy ass White people!*

She parks her car into an abandoned driveway and then follows in pursuit. With every step Deja took, getting closer and closer to them, her heart races and her breathing was fast.

Now close to them, the guy turns around in enough time for Deja to punch him in the nose. As he falls down, Deja grabs the girlfriend and covers her mouth before she can scream; she didn't put up much of a fight either.

"Please don't hurt us! We'll give you whatever you want!" the boyfriend says.

"Give me your fucking wallet! I want all the money out of it!" Deja says with a deep voice, masking over hers.

She watches as the boyfriend gets out his wallet and tosses it at Deja's feet. She forces the girlfriend to pick it up and go through it for his money, collecting fifty dollars. Deja wanted to curse at the small amount of money to get from him, but takes the money and releases the girl. Allowing the man to keep his wallet, she runs off as fast as she can.

Deja left the area, her heart throbbing hard through her chest, and the radio volume off. She was better off stealing money from where she worked at; stealing just a measly fifty bucks from that couple.

Fifty dollars got Deja some gas in her tank, a pack of cigarettes and a cold beer leaving her less than thirty dollars in her pocket. With a free weekend night the next day, Deja was ready to do it all over again.

She found herself going back for more, getting up to only two hundred dollars and some change. She got that money so quick, right before her next paycheck, adding extra to it.

Sitting kicked back on the bed with a cold can of Modelo beer in her hand and a cigarette in the other, they were all watching the BET channel. The actress playing the mother was a high paid escort and her daughter wanted her to straighten her life up. Deja had reached an idea in her head. What if she could lure rich men into another hotel room, somewhere fancy and rob them after she drugs them? Nope, that's not her cup of tea.

Like the thief she is, Deja waited until her kids were still asleep to leave the room in the middle of the night. She didn't target innocent and young White couples or houses; she went for their cars. With a different wig, mask and gloves on, Deja went from car to car, checking their doors and trunks.

If they were unlock, she'd fish and ramble through the glove compartment or under the armrest, typical spots where cards or money could be stashed away. One guy was stupid enough to leave his wallet in the car with a credit card and a hundred dollars inside it. If only she knew the pin to it. Another person left things she could take and sell at a pawn shop. And then there was one guy that left a whole bag of money in the back of his trunk, stopping Deja in her tracks.

Deja lifted her mask, catching her breath from rambling. She couldn't believe she had really come up on a duffle bag of money. "This can't be real cash," she says and pulls her mask down over her face.

She took one stack of hundreds, removing the thin piece of paper that held them together. Deja read the number 10,000 on the small paper. She touches and feels the money for herself to see is it real. She ain't never ran across something like this before. After stuffing it all down between her shirt and camisole, Deja grabbed another stack that was a total of a thousand, it was smaller than the first one.

Deja was in the greatest relief and heaven until she hears footsteps quickly approaching her. Without closing the trunk, she went low and moved from the trunk to the rear side of the car, hearing the footsteps stop on the other side of the vehicle. Holding her breath, she looks underneath the car, spotting a pair of feet. *Oh shit!* She can't afford to be caught, then it's jail and time away from her kids! They wouldn't understand waking up to her not being there.

"I know you're out here somewhere! Give up now

before I call the police," he says, loudly taking his next step. She didn't want to, but she reaches inside her jacket pocket for her knife. No one and nothing is going to come in the way. She'll take the whole damn bag and get the fuck out of town with her kids and the money! This is for the birds!

Deja turns to the rear of the car and whistles, drawing the man towards her direction. Following the sound, he walks towards the rear of the car. Deja stands up and jabs her knife at him, meeting her match. Strong and tall, the guy countered her hand and then twists her wrist with the knife in it, forcing her to drop it. Deja briefly screams and rams her head into his, making them both pull away and stumble back. Using what she knows, Deja crouches and then swoops her leg underneath the guy. He falls to the ground with a loud cry. She prances on top of him, pinning his arms down with her kneecaps and then retrieving her knife again.

"Please! Please!" the man screams repeatedly. Deja could've went psycho and stabbed the hell out of him, but she pounded his face with her fists instead.

A gunshot was fired in the air, making her stop and look back. "Get off of him now!" a man orders, emerging from the darkness with a double barrel in his hands, aiming it at her.

With her hands in the air, Deja slowly stands up and then turns to face the shooter. "You're going to shoot a woman?" she calmly asks him.

"You're not a woman, you're an intruder and you're on my property. Get up, Trevor!" he orders the other guy. "Drop the knife now!"

Deja obediently releases the knife from her hand. She watches as Trevor quickly runs past her and join the man. "We gotta call the police."

"How much did you take from me, huh?" the man asks her.

Deja didn't understand why he was asking her such a question. He was better off calling the police cause she's not talking.

"Take that mask off!" he then orders her, moving closer.

"You're being too nice! She tried to kill me!" Trevor whines from behind them. "Thieves don't need a reason to take what they want! They just do."

Deja removes her mask and wig once the guy holds the mouth of the gun to her chest. She doesn't break down and cry right away, but Deja held the tears in her eyes and her brows pressed together. *It's over with for her? Or is it?*

"Now you can call the police," the man says, still holding her at gunpoint. Deja saw an opportunity to run with a fifty percent chance that he'd miss her, and that's what she did.

Quickly scooping up the knife, Deja swiftly turns around and then takes off running. The man fired off one shot, missing her as she predicted until she reached the end of the large open gates, where he fired again. The rock salt that hit the fence had splattered and splashed when Deja reached the other side, getting into her left eye.

Screaming and hollering, Deja continues running, rubbing her now irritated and burning left eye while using her right eye to see!

"Get the car!" the man ordered the other one. She ran faster until she reaches her car, and then gets in, but doesn't crank it up. Laying back low in the rear seat, Deja bid her time and wait. Her left eye is hurting so bad and she did her best not to cry. It felt like something was trying to pick her eye out, bit by bit.

She then spotted them; the Trevor guy was walking as the other was driving in his car. "Shit!" she hisses, seeing Trevor stop and look at her car parked in someone else driveway. He remain standing still, observing the car, trying to see could it be her.

From time to time, these houses have family members visiting and would park their cars just like Deja had. After no sign of movement, his suspension was gone and he continued walking. Deja sighed in relief and then exits her car, watching them drive and walk away until they disappear around the corner.

She moves quick, cranking up her car and driving normally with her money and her eye hurting like hell!

Once she was clear and out the area, she couldn't take it anymore and went to the ER. Deja was lucky to still have her eye and her life. The nurses went asking questions and the only thing Deja could say was that she was caught in a line of fire, being an innocent bystander and she didn't remember the guy's faces.

She returned to her motel later than expected, seeing her kids already awake. They all had walked to the corner store to get themselves something to eat while she was away. Once her two oldest kids seen her eye, she was bombarded with their questions.

"Ma, what happened to your eye? Who did that to you? Where you been?" Marterrio asks her.

"You didn't catch up with Big Doug did you?" Raine asks her.

"She had better not!" Marterrio interjects.

"No, I'm okay and hell no I didn't catch back up to that nigga, but we have to go now. We're leaving town today," she firmly says.

"Wait? Now? Where are we going?" Raine asks.

"Somewhere we can live. Now let's go," Deja moves over to the other side of the room and grabs a bag.

In thirty minutes, they had their things and loaded it all into Deja's car trunk. She could only think of one place where she could go to and thrive; back to her old hometown in the bluff city.

Chapter 2

After driving for nearly four hours straight in the dead of night, on the highway, Deja's eyes were finally heavy. She was resistant towards going to sleep, knowing that they were almost close to home.

The pavement was smoothly running underneath her car, the radio volume turned low with the humming sound of her daughters gently snoring in the backseat. The only ones left awake were Deja and Marterrio.

"Ma, are you going to tell me what happened to your eye?"

"No," she simply replies, her eyes still on the road. Now she's awake.

"Dad was telling me one time that you used to have a problem with not stealing. He said you'd rack up lots of money doing it. Is he right?"

"Marterrio, he's completely wrong, because I'm not that woman anymore. That was before I had you and it's history now. You have nothing to worry about," she calmly says, reassuring him. Marterrio gave her the side eye like he wasn't falling for it.

"And your eye? Why there's a patch over it?"

"Marterrio, it's disrespectful to ask adults certain questions. If I tell you that you have nothing to worry about then that's what the fuck I mean?" she snaps at him.

"Okay ma," he turns his head away and watches the miles of land outstretching over the highway.

In the next forty minutes, they had finally made it into the city. Everyone was either asleep or coming in from work this time of the night.

Deja came right from the highway and then onto the interstate, taking the exit ramp off of Shelby Drive. She drove down Raines and into the Westwood area where her Aunt Yvette house was. Aunt Yvette lives in her peaceful home made of stone with four bedrooms and three bathrooms and no one bothers her.

There was one incident with her husband when she had to let the neighborhood know not to fuck with her or her property. Ever since, no one messed with her aunt Yvette or whoever comes around her house.

Deja was so happy to pull up in the driveway with her kids and the few things they had with them. She called her Aunt's cell phone and then waits for her to pick up.

"Hello?" Aunt Yvette voice sleepily answers the phone.

"Aunt Yvette," Deja says.

"Deja baby? This you?" she says, sounding more alert and woke now.

"Yea, it's me. I'm outside with my kids, and it's late. Can you come and open the door for us?"

"H-h-how late is it?" Aunt Yvette asks her. Deja sighs and leans her head into the steering wheel. She had reached another moment where she wanted to fold and cry again, but not here.

"Please Aunt Yvette. Just let us lay our heads here for

17

the night and I'll think of somewhere else for us to go," Deja pleads with her.

"Oh, no. It's all good, baby. I didn't see the time. Here I come, okay?" she says and then hangs up.

Deja wasn't expecting Aunt Yvette to come to the door. She was expecting for her aunt to not open her door for her and her kids, forcing her to turn her back on her family forever, but Aunt Yvette didn't.

With it being so late in the morning and tired from the long drive, Deja could've slept in. When you got to get to where you're going, there's no time for complete rest.

Despite them all showing up on her porch step at the crack of dawn, Aunt Yvette was the first to rise out of bed and handle her hygiene in the bathroom. First she started her coffee and then she began making breakfast. She ain't cooked like this in a long time since the family used to meet up over her house for her husband's birthday dinner or some other family function.

Aunt Yvette knew Deja's history and she was never the perfect kind of child coming up. Deja always used to get into trouble, whether at school or in hot water with her mom. That girl stayed rebelling against her mom's rules, but Deja did graduate with an honors diploma and made it to be in the top ten of her classmates. She was bad, but very intelligent as well.

And when she turned 18, Deja couldn't wait to leave her mom's house and try to bring hell Aunt Yvette's way. She said hell to the no and made Deja get a job. That worked out for so long until her niece was caught selling dope, becoming a juvenile delinquent. The only Aunt Yvette did for Deja is let her experience life and all its woes and joys on her own, and then she left town.

Biscuits, cheddar grits, baked bacon, and with a side of eggs, breakfast was complete. Waiting in the kitchen near the window, drinking her cup of warm coffee, Aunt Yvette glances to the right to see Deja enter the room. She dragged her feet a little as she walked and her hair was messy.

"Did you at least wash your face?" Aunt Yvette asks her.

"I did that and brushed my teeth. Good morning to you too, Aunt Yvette," she walks over to the counter and pours herself a cup of coffee.

"So what are you doing back, huh?"

"I got involved with the wrong man and lost my apartment. So now I'm here to start over," Deja sighs, now having a sudden urge to smoke a cigarette.

"Girl, how in the hell do you lose your government assisted apartment? And why you got that patch over your eye?" Aunt Yvette ponders with a fixed look on her face. "Help me understand that?"

"I had dealings with the wrong nigga, that's all you need to know," Deja rolls her eyes and then glares out the window.

"Well, I'm here if you need me, but what are you going to do? School is about to start soon and you have to get your paperwork together. Have you decided where you'll work at?"

"I know it's going to be a process but I have it all figured out, Aunt Yvette. We just needed somewhere to temporarily lay our heads at," Deja sternly says, her gaze returning back to Aunt Yvette.

There was no words to say to each other. Getting her car and papers right with the state of Tennessee was a process. With the money that she stole, Deja was able put down enough money for a two bedroom duplex and furnish it with decent, used furniture. That money was a big blessing for Deja and her kids. She wanted to make sure that she didn't over spend, and stored the rest in a bank account.

Finding somewhere decent to live was better than where they were at, but the real struggle is always trying to find a nice job. No one would too much hire Deja with her background, but a warehouse. In the day she did ten hours inside a nearly hot climate warehouse for nine dollars an hour, and by night, Deja became a servant for one of those restaurants near the riverfront.

A job like her evening job always had the large tips. She's not that old, but in her early, middle thirties with a young spirited face. Deja knew how to have a conversation with a customer whether they were by themselves or with someone else. She knew how to smile and make people feel comfortable, and that's what earned Deja her tips.

It was after one in the morning like how it'd always be when Deja would get off from work. Parking her car along the rough edged driveway, Deja could see by looking at the windows that the living room, kitchen and bathroom lights were all on, which should be off this time of night.

"The hell these kids got going on?" she says to herself, exiting her car. Tired and worn out, Deja gently closes her car door and then makes her way up the pavement side-walk. After turning her key in the iron security door, it hardly makes any noise when she opened it.

Deja had a feeling that she wouldn't be able to find the bed fast enough, but she was hoping like hell that her kids had her house together. Now opening the wooden door with an easy push, someone had loudly gasped. Deja's eyes quickly looked in the direction the gasp came from to see someone's bald headed, teenage daughter sitting on the lap of her son.

"What the hell?" Deja says, frowning to see them on her couch! The girl didn't have anything decent on,

20

wearing a tank top and short jean skirt. "Oh hell no! It smell like some two week old tuna salad up in here. Girl, who is your momma?" Deja remains standing at the door, blocking its entry.

"I don't even have a momma," the girl says, straightening her clothes.

Deeply thinking, Deja eyes went from the girl and to Marterrio. She fights like hell to keep him out of trouble and on the right path, but he just won't get right. Suckling her teeth, Deja says, "You get your lil overkill, tuna pussy smelling ass out of my house and don't come back unless you come to me to be invited in my shit like a real woman!"

"Damn ma!" Marterrio says. Deja moves to the side, allowing the girl to leave who runs out the door. Marterrio sighs and smooths his hand over his head from back to front.

"For real? That's all you got to say to me is damn? What the fuck is she doing in my house, Marterrio?"

"What does it look like? We were cuddling," he says and then sighs. Gritting her teeth, Deja's blood boils as she gets the urge to make her hand into a tight fist. She restrains herself from fighting Marterrio. There's a better way to deal with him.

"Y'all were cuddling my ass! Don't have that girl in my house no more when I'm not around," Deja firmly says.

"I heard you," Marterrio gets up from the couch and walks into the hallway. Deja sighs and walks into her kitchen. Disappointed, she grits her teeth and then turns around; of course it isn't clean. Dishes were in the sink, trash wasn't taken out and they had left their unfinished plates on the table like there's a maid around to come and get it?

"Wake up! Come on, get your ass up!" Deja rushes into

the bedroom her oldest kids shared together; little Rylee slept in the bed with her. She flickers the light switch on, and then goes over to the full twin size bed that Raine was asleep on. Marterrio hadn't closed his eyes yet, immediately sitting up.

"Ma! What is you doing? She got school in the morning," he fumes.

"Go and look at my kitchen! Y'all need to get up and figure it out!" Deja angrily snatches the covers off from Raine. Disoriented, Raine pops up from her sleep, slowly blinking her eyes.

"Ma," Raine sleepily calls, holding her arm up from the light rays.

"Mane you tripping," Marterrio says.

"If you don't like it here, Marterrio, you can go back to Georgia and be some random girl pushover!" Deja snaps at him.

"I would have but you stopped me cause your dumbass let some fat slob come in and play with the rent money!" Marterrio bad mouths her, almost raising his voice. He seen the quick anger in his mom's eyes and knew it was too late to take back what he said.

"Ma! Mom!" Raine was shouting, seeing that her mom had just jumped on her brother. Deja had Marterrio by the neck. He grips her at the waist to lift her up, but Deja kicks the bed and down to the floor they both went. "Stop it!" Raine now yells as they were scuffling and flipping around until their mom pins Marterrio down.

Hearing Raine crying, Deja points her hand at her and orders her, "Now you shut up! Stop all that damn crying! All y'all have to do is clean my house while I'm at work. It's not hard to do. You wanna talk back and have females in my house that you don't even know, you can find the door

22

or do as I say!" Deja catches her breath, and then turns her attention to Raine.

"Don't ever leave my kitchen like the way y'all did tonight. I shouldn't have to come home to a nasty ass kitchen when I have a house with two big ass teenagers! Y'all live, eat, shit and sleep in this motherfucker just as much as I do. I expect my house to be -" Deja stops talking to see Raine still crying and shaking her head.

"Girl, what you still crying for?" Deja finally gets up and stands straight.

"Because you're always fighting all the time," she cries, wiping her eyes dry. "You've fought dad. You've fought two of your boyfriends, and now you're fighting Marterrio. You're angry all the time, mom."

"I'm not angry all the time," Deja argues. "I expect shit from people and I get let down every time. You'd be angry sometimes too. Now y'all need to get my kitchen cleaned up."

With a glass of wine in one hand and a cigarette in the other, Deja sat in the living room with the TV off and the sound of Marterrio and Raine straightening up the kitchen. She reflects on her childhood. Raine gave her something to think about. Deja never ran across a fight or moment to fight that she didn't turn away from. Luckily, assault wasn't a charge that was a part of her background.

Lying asleep in her warm bed from the dullness of the heat that barely kept the house warm, Deja was deep in her sleep when a large splatter of cold water pours onto her. She wakes up from out of her sleep, her hair wet, and her heart racing. Deja didn't understand what just happened until she looks right at the smug glare on her mom's face.

"What did I do wrong?" Deja whines at her mom, her voice breaking. She tried her best to keep from crying.

"You forgot to wash them motherfucking dishes in my sink, Deja.

I told you what was going to happen if I came home and you didn't have my sink clean! Get your ass up!" her mom bends down and then grabs Deja by her whole arm.

"Ouch! You're hurting me! Mom please!" she cries out. Her mom is ten times stronger than she, and Deja wished like hell she could fight her mom off. Her breath smelled of alcohol with another bad odor.

As she pulls and forced Deja into the living room, she spots a crack pipe on the table before her mom continues to pull her away.

"Please!" Deja cries, now being shoved over the threshold and into the night, cold and crisp air! Her mom quickly closes the door before Deja could regain her balance.

"Mom! Please! It's wet and I'm cold," Deja cries at the door, her right fists clutching together, her wet hair exposed making her extra cold. Deja felt like she was in a windstorm!

There was a lot of things she hated about her mom more than the small things she loved about her. She always finds some sort of way to abuse Deja, especially when she's high and drunk. It's like hurting her made her mom feel good about herself because she had someone to boss around.

"You better learn how to clean my motherfucking house then, bitch! And do it the right way, don't half ass around. I'ma leave you out there long enough so it won't happen again!" her mom loudly spoke from the other side of the door.

Cold and shivering, Deja was able to make it from her mom's house and to the nearest gas station, drawing attention to herself. While there was a woman that called for help, Deja called for her Aunt Yvette to come and get her.

A nice woman on her way home from work had let Deja sit in her car and warm up, but her vehicle heat wasn't hot enough. Aunt Yvette had arrived thirty minutes late with a torn look on her face. Deja was still shivering; she even broke out crying to see her aunt.

"Oh, baby! It's alright, I'm here now. Come on. Thank you, ma'am," Aunt Yvette says to the woman.

"Hey, I called child protective services. May I get your contact info to give them?"

"No the hell you may not," Aunt Yvette stops walking as she snaps the woman up.

"This baby came to me with her hair and shirt wet, and it's below forty degrees out here, ma'am," the woman stands her ground.

"Understand, this child is almost eighteen years old. Whatever that's going on is between my family and them only. Now I said thank you, but this is as far as your nosey ass knows. Come on, baby," wrapping her arm around Deja's shoulders, the two of them walk away.

Deja sat by the fireplace, rays of steam rising from her mug of hot chocolate untouched, and her hair was finally dry. Aunt Yvette sat perched on the recliner chair, slowly sipping from her mug of hot chocolate.

"Deja?" she calls with her low and motherly voice.

"Who pours cold water on their daughter and then puts her in the cold?" Deja says, dropping her head towards the floor. Shaking her head from side to side, Deja pauses for a minute and then releases a cry. That's something she can't get over.

"Your mom wasn't always this bad. She'd have her days, but I wouldn't think she was capable of abusing her own child," Aunt Yvette quietly spoke over the cackles of the fire.

"So you're excusing her now? What's next? She's going to beat my back in and you're still gonna take up for her?" Deja asks and then pulls herself together.

"Well, Deja, until you're 18, you are your mother's full responsibility. You gotta stop cutting up and do what she says. That's all she wants," Aunt Yvette was calm and trying to explain her mom's actions, but they weren't justifiable enough for Deja. With her eyes fixed on the embers of the flames, she didn't comprehend a word her aunt just said.

25

ANGRY AND IN RAGE, Deja shoves the door open, her mom was hot on her heels right behind her. "You bring your ass back here!" her mom shouts after Deja.

She quickly moves across the unkept green yard and over to Jayceon's black, Chevrolet Camero as he gets out of his car. "Don't bring no shit to my car, Deja!" he calmly says to her.

"It's not me! It's her!" Deja snaps at him. She takes a deep breath and then says, "You know what? Forget this! I'll walk, nigga! Fuck both of y'all!" Deja threw up her hand in the air and storms off from her boyfriend and mom.

"Where are you going, huh? Nobody's gonna take you in! You low life bitch!" her mom taunts her, going after Deja.

Deja twirls around on her heels and then wait for her mom to catch up to her. "I don't have to live with you or him!" she says, tears filling her eyes, her nostrils flared open. "I'm 18 years old now. I won't be your rag doll anymore, you crazy, junkie ass hoe!"

Deja's mom raises her hand and then slaps Deja. After tasting blood in her mouth, Deja and her mom breaks out into a brawl in the middle of the street.

Jayceon rushes over to pull them apart. Deja had her mom gripped by her hair with one hand and her other arm wrapped around her mom's neck! She never looked forward to fighting her mother until now. Deja couldn't take no more of her disrespect!

"Get off her, girl! That's your mom!" Jayceon finally plucks Deja off her mom.

"You little juvenile delinquent! I'm calling the police on you! You better have your bond money," her mom threatens her, holding her aching head in her hand. She runs away as Deja tears free from Jayceon. He chases her down and then restrains Deja again, yelling in her ear, "Get your crazy ass in the car, mane!"

Watching her mom go into the house, Deja and Jayceon quickly gets inside the car and then he sped off into the night.

"Where do you have in mind to go, huh, Deja? Cause I'm still trying to get my place," Jayceon says.

"I'll go to my Aunt!" she yells at him. "Why do you care?"

"Cause you're my girl and I don't want to see you messed up out here! You're eighteen and ain't even graduated yet, mane. Finish high school first, crazy ass! Then you get a job so you can have some money. You work that job, clock in and stay to yourself and go home, hell," he suggests her, and then exhales.

Deja did that… as fast as she graduated, she ended up being pregnant and living with her Aunt Yvette. Jayceon still didn't have a place for them to go and that's when life got real for them both.

At their end, they sat in the front seat of Jayceon's car with their meals from Burger King and their one month old son in the backseat asleep. Deja's eyes were fixed on the calm flow of the Mississippi River. They had been sleeping in a motel room since Deja gave birth now.

Sighing, Jayceon says, "Let's get out of here."

"What do you mean?" Deja calmly asks him.

"Think about it, baby. Your aunt halfway don't want to help and I don't have my family to help me. Let's roll, Deja! Let's relocate and live somewhere else. Let's start over again, cause this city ain't working for neither of us," he then glances back at the car seat in the backseat.

He had a point. They had finally hit rock bottom and the only way out was to go up together. "Let's do it then. Let's go," Deja reaches over and holds his hand in hers.

"You for real?" Jayceon glares at Deja in her eyes. Deja reaches over and holds his free hand in hers and says, "Let's go."

"MOM?" Raine's voice says from across the room, breaking her memories. Deja looks in her direction. "The kitchen's clean," Raine later says. Deja waves her hand at her in dismissal, her cigarette burned down to the butt and her glass now empty.

27

Deja made sure that she had washed her glass after herself and then went to bed.

The following morning, getting Rylee ready for school, Deja receive a phone call from an out of state number. Deeply sighing, she answers the phone and says, "Hello?"

"Um…hey there," Reese's voice says on the other end.

"What do you want?"

"I want you to stop being mad at me and start being an adult, Deja. I've been trying to get in touch with you for weeks about my girls now," he says. Her eyes went over to Rylee, who was searching for her White girl school shoes.

"Well we moved back home to Memphis."

"Since when?"

"We been here for weeks now, Reese," she answers him.

"Well you pulled a fast one on me. Do they need anything?"

"No," she replies, her pride always getting in the way. It was hard on her pockets taking care of Raine these days now that she's a teenager. Raine wants to stay in the inner circle and keep up with the latest fashion trends. It wouldn't be right for her to get in the way of Reese providing for his daughters.

"But hold on. I'm going to let you talk to Raine and see what she got going on," Deja says.

"Okay, cool," he says on the other end.

Deja walks from her bedroom and down the short hallway that lead to Raine's room. Just as Deja barges in and opens the door, Raine is gawking at her reflection in the dresser mirror. Seeing her mom come in, she stops checking out her physique and then gasps, "Mom."

"Your dad's on the phone," Deja says to her with her hand extended out. As Raine quickly pulls on her white uniform shirt and then gets the phone, Deja leaves the room to let her have her privacy.

On their drive to school, Deja had to ask Raine. "So, how was your conversation with your dad? What y'all talked about?"

"You talked to daddy?" Rylee curiously asks Raine.

"Yes and it was cool. He said that he misses us and to ask you can we go to his house when we're on fall break. So can we?" Raine asks.

"I don't know y'all," Deja shrugs her shoulders. "I don't know that woman he married. I don't know what type of woman she is or if she'll feel some type of way with you two around her husband."

"If she makes dad happy, I'm pretty sure she's not even like that," Raine says, her tone low and calm.

"You're just a child and you don't understand some things about grown people and life, but your dad hasn't been knowing that woman long enough to marry her and bring y'all around."

"They been together for a year now, mom. And she knows us."

"My answer is no," Deja's tone was firm and she sighs. "Did you need anything and tell him?"

"I wanted some money to eat and stuff, that's all," Raine turns away and looks out the window. They left the conversation alone and remained quiet for the rest of their drive.

Chapter 3

Fast asleep after working two shifts and pulling an extra hour on both, Deja thought she was dreaming when there was a loud knock on the front door. Stirred and concerned, Deja immediately wakes up from out of her sleep, her heart racing fast. The knock was harder. She hurries out of bed, across the bedroom floor to the hallway and then right into the living room.

Without even thinking, Deja opens the front door, nearly pushed over by Marterrio as he comes raging in. Hot with sweat dripping down his face and his clothes moist, Marterrio grabs his mom by the arms and says, "Mom! I need your help! Don't ask me questions. Just take this!" Releasing her, Marterrio reaches down into his pockets with both hands, one of them pulling money out and then the other filled full of dope.

Deja's mind was still waking up, so she couldn't grasp what was going on or voice her opinion! All she could think about was how his father came to her the same way when Marterrio was just a year old. Marterrio places the dope and money into her hands.

30

"Son -" were the only words she could make of, hearing sirens blaring in the distance.

"You have to hide it so they won stick it to me, ma! Please!" his eyes were wide with fear as he glances at her. Quickly nodding her head, Deja rushes away as Marterrio lingers behind in the living room. She thought fast, going into the kids room and then straight over to Rylee's favorite stuffed animal. What other place to hide Marterrio's drugs than her old place?

Once she hid the drugs in the stuffed animal, Deja was running out of time as the police arrives outside in front of her duplex, their bright blue lights flashing past the thin curtains over the windows in the living room. Deja now runs over to the fuel box, opening its thin metal door and storing the cash right into a small slot in the wood that a rat would use for entry.

As there was a loud knock at the door, Deja closes the fuel box door and then runs back into the living room. Marterrio was standing near the front door and about to open it, but Deja couldn't stop her son. She couldn't save him this go round from his bad deeds; they had caught up with him.

She watches from the living room floor in awe as Marterrio willingly surrenders to the surrounding police officers. There was more than three officers and they had long barrel guns aiming them at her baby! Deja didn't understand why it takes four squad cars to six officers for one teenager.

"Please, don't hurt him! He's just a kid! Don't handle my son like that!" Deja was fuming at one cop who had his knee pierced down into Marterrio's back as they had him on the ground and handcuffing him.

"Stay back ma'am," one officer orders her. As a cop

31

had now rushed past her, one thing was happening too fast before the other.

"My girls are in there asleep!" Deja tries to go after him until the closest officer near her, grabs her arm.

"He has to check your house just in case of any evidence, ma'am," he firmly says. Deja frowns at him, wanting to snatch her arm away from the officer. "Meanwhile, I have a few questions to ask you," he says, guiding her away from the living room, to outside.

Answering the officer's questions, Deja was watching them from the side of her eye as they escorted Marterrio into the first squad car, pushing his head down on his way in. She bit down onto her lip, restraining herself from being angry and speaking out of place as well as crying. Deja scratches her head and then sighs, holding her tears in her eyes.

"Excuse me, I don't mean to be rude, but please don't kill my son," she says, changing their conversation. The White officer stood with a perplexed look on his face at her.

"Ma'am..." he was speechless.

Tears filled her eyes, and with a firm tone, Deja says again, "I said please don't murder my son. I'm trusting you all to deliver him to be booked at 201 Poplar alive. I see what's happening on the news every day to black boys and men."

"Ms. Allen, that's not what we do, but I'll make sure he's safe and doesn't bring any harm to himself and others," he says.

"He's not a mad man," she then rolls her eyes as the officer that searched her house approached them. Deja wipes her eyes dry before her tears could fall.

"Find anything?" the other one in front of her asks him. He shook his head and then continues walking away.

Deja couldn't breathe until she seen their flashing lights disappear into the night. She did something she hadn't done in a long time. Fell down on her knees and prayed for some sort of sign; what did her son do wrong? Why was he out selling dope and where?

In three more hours, Deja had to go in to work or make another choice; take off from her job and see her son. She would go back to sleep, but it wouldn't work because her thoughts wouldn't allow her.

Two hours after, a taunting number had called Deja's phone. She had let the number call again twice to see would it call back in less than the thirty minutes she estimated.

"Hello?" she answers right away.

"Hello, you have a collect call from 'Marterrio', an inmate here at the Shelby County Jail Facility. All calls are being monitored. Press zero to answer or otherwise, hang up," the automated voice says. Sighing, Deja pressed zero on the touch screen.

"Mom," Marterrio says on the other end.

She was now fully awoke just to fuss at him. "Boy, what did you do? Why wasn't your ass in the bed last night?"

"I'm sorry mom," Marterrio says. "Will you come and see me in lower level before they take me up?"

"Do you know how much your bond is boy?" Deja asks him, narrowing her eyes. She then sighs again.

"No, I won't be arraigned until tomorrow morning... well in a couple of more hours and find out then. You're gonna get me out of here?" he asks her.

"You damn right I am, and then I'm going to kick your ass! In Georgia, you got away with your bullshit that you pulled when you broke in them folks' cars! I'm not going to spare your ass this go round. Don't you know that you're messing up your record? Ain't nobody gonna want to hire your black ass when you turn 19 and have a dope charge or a burglary charge!"

"I know! I know, mom. I'll do whatever I can to not end up here again, I promise," he says.

"You have five minutes!" the automated voice cuts into the phone's mic before Deja could say what's next on her mind.

Sitting at the table, suckling her teeth with one arm crossed under her elbow, Deja nods her head and says, "Mhm, I know damn well you will."

"I love you mom," he says before the call ends.

She couldn't fold how she wanted to; Marterrio had to be a big boy about his arrest. Deja had called in to work and stayed at the house. She did something she only had time to do on the weekends, cook and make breakfast. What else could she do to get her mind off her son?

One dish at a time, Deja whipped together a pot of grits, and biscuits were in the stove as well with the sausages that were cooking also. Lastly, Deja had baked the bacon. By the time breakfast was done, the girls had woke up right on cue. Drinking her mug of warm coffee with an urge to smoke a cigarette, Deja watches as her daughters went straight in and ate their breakfast. She doesn't bother to tell them a thing.

Like every morning, they all exited the house at one time, but her routine was different. Instead of going straight to work, Deja took the I-240 to downtown.

Before entering, she already knew the do's and don't's. Deja smoked half a cigarette before leaving her car.

The wait wasn't long after she signed in. It kind of felt like yesterday since she last seen him.

Marterrio sat on the opposite side of the thick glass partition while Deja sat in the stool on the other side. She had no worries seeing that his face was unscathed.

34

"Did you find out how much your bond is yet?" she asks him.

"It's one thousand," he says with a grin on his face.

"This shit is not a game out here, Marterrio. Some young niggas get flapped by the police one time and that's all it takes! And you're a minor," she frowns at him. Deja checks around her, seeing if the other two women were paying her any attention to the way she was talking.

Lowering her tone, she says, "Once you're in the system, you're always in the system. You'll be a six digit number to them or a boy! Your name won't be Marterrio Howard. That motherfucker gone be inmate 560621."

Marterrio holds his head down and gently shakes it from it side to side. "I know mom. I'm going to straighten up and try to find somewhere to work when I'm out of here," he says.

"Yea, we'll see. Just hang on tight. I'm going to go and make your bond now," she stands up and then walks away.

Deja didn't hear again from Marterrio until he was released from jail in the latest hour of the night. She still couldn't believe what he did.

"Ma," Marterrio's voice is low and cautious. Deja didn't answer him, but waited for Marterrio to say what's on his mind. She wanted to beat the hell out of him. "I need a lawyer for my next court date."

"What they hit you with?" her tone was blunt and firm.

"Just for evading arrest. They're really mad because they knew I had drugs but could find any," he proudly brags with a grin.

"Damn, do you think this shit is a game out here? Cause it's not! And the next time you get caught up, I'm not bailing you out," Deja fussed at him. While Marterrio had every right in his mind to feel that Deja is right, she now felt like that maybe moving to Memphis was a bad idea. Deja isn't around, and neither are their dads to keep Marterrio or Raine in check.

"And I'm damn sure not stashing away your drug money and drugs!" she later adds. "We're burning that shit when we get back to the house."

"No, ma! You don't understand! You can't burn it," he pleads with her.

"Why the hell not?!"

"Because it's not my money. I'm just like the middle guy! Those are not my drugs and half of that money isn't mine," he explains as Deja sat in the driver seat shaking her head from side to side.

"How much more you owe?" she asks him.

"Just what I have, but I have to sell the rest of the drugs."

Deja said she'd never touch drugs and the dirty money it involves again, but she found herself in a predicament to save her son, giving her no choice. Like old times and with Marterrio's contact list, Deja sold off all the rest of the drugs. By the time she was done, it was time to take the girls to school, and she had called in on her morning job again.

"So where the plug at?" Deja now asks her son, standing in the doorway between the living room and the hallway.

"That man ain't gonna want to see you," Marterrio says with acid in his tone. "Them folks gone look at me like a boy!"

"You are a boy! You ain't even 18 years old yet and you already about to catch a drug charge in the system, child! Nobody gonna wanna hire a street level drug dealer nor rent out an apartment to you either! Now where this motherfucker at?" she snaps at him. Sighing, sitting on the couch and feeling uneasy, Marterrio smooths his hands over his head.

Just what Deja thought, the plug was some old head nigga trapping out of one of those shot gun houses in South Memphis. Shot gun houses are the vacant homes you see that have the boards over the windows, but you see a car or two parked in the yard a certain time of day. It's far from a trap house.

Embarrassed, Marterrio slumps down into the passenger seat, watching from the side of his eye as his mom strolls up the sidewalk. There were two junkies lingering on the porch, one female and one male. Deja gently shakes her head; it's too early in the day to be getting high.

"Hey baby, what's good," the junkie guy says, swaying from side to side as if he was doing the two step dance.

"Where the fuck is Cane?" she asks him.

"Damn baby! You ain't gotta be all hostile! You can deal with me. Fuck Cane," the junkie says, stretching his arms out wide as the female laughs and cackles, musk and funk coming from his arm wind making Deja snarl her nose at him.

The old wooden door pulls open, and a tall, muscular toned man emerges from the house and then steps out onto the porch. With a strong body physique, a sleeve of tattoos down both arms, and a low fade haircut, the man storms over to the junkie guy first.

"Aye! Y'all two need to get the fuck on from around here!" he threatens them.

Deja stands out of the way and watches as the man first tosses the guy into the lawn and then shoved the woman down the three porch steps.

"Damn motherfucker! You big ole, black hulk!" the guy curses at the big man.

He then pulls out a Glock with a long barrel and says, "Move some!" His eyes didn't meet Deja's until the two were gone. They left the yard talking shit.

"What's up? What you want?" he snaps at her.

"Who's Cane?" she asks.

"Hold up, shorty. You just can't come around here asking for me like that. Who is you? You tryna buy some?"

"No, you can't be talking to me like I'm one of these lil ass girls on your level. I found something I think belongs to you through word of mouth," she firmly says. Peeping out the situation, Cane glares past Deja, spotting the top of Marterrio's head that was trying to hide in the passenger seat. Cane chuckles and invites Deja inside.

There was hardly any furniture in the living room except for a chest cooler, a chair next to a table with drugs stashed on the top of it. The wood interior smells old and the floorboards creaked every time they took a step or walked. Standing adjacent to each other, Cane counts the money one dollar bill at a time. His brows pressed together as Deja watches him.

"Damn, ma. You know what you doing, huh? Sold dope before?" he jokingly asks her, placing the money back.

"That's none of your business. My son won't be slanging for you anymore," she firmly says, as they now made eye contact with each other.

"You feisty," he taunts her.

"You heard what I said."

"You can't control him, *mom*. Your boy been got a taste of these hot ass streets. I mean excuse my French," he says.

Standing her ground, Deja takes one step close to Cane and then says, "I might can't control him, but he's my son. I'll do anything to save him. Now I'm out of here."

"Yea, aight. Can I get your number, *mom?*" he jokes with Deja and then cackles as she continues walking away.

After exiting the old smelling house, Deja deeply exhales and then walks faster towards her car. Like the kid he was, Marterrio sat in her car with his lip poked out and his face frowning. For the hell of it, Deja takes her hand and pops Marterrio aside the back of his head.

"Ow! What you do that for?" he exclaims.

"Because that nigga is a asshole and he too damn grown to see you out here dealing drugs! He should be telling you to do some' positive with your life. You out here being stupid and shit!" she fussed at him and then finally cranks up her car. "I done missed two days of work from my first job for your ass. Don't do this shit no more. I'm gone kick your ass, Marterrio! I'm not playing," she warns him and drives off from the curb.

Deja was lucky to still have her first job after calling in for two days straight. For the hell of it, her supervisor made her job harder, putting almost all of the work load on Deja. Then it came time to work her second job when she just wanted to give up.

With her kids not around, locked in the restroom with just herself, Deja silently sobs until she pulls herself together. Running the paper towel under warm water, she dabs it underneath her eyes and then checks her reflection.

Exiting the restroom, Deja's eyes were down on the floor when she wasn't paying attention. Before she could hold her head up, she had collided with someone big. Something cold and wet had spilled onto her shirt, also nearly knocking the air out of her. Losing her balance and focus, Deja stumbles back. She was about to fall until a strong grip grabs her by the arm and then pulls her into a firm chest.

"Are you alright?" his deep voice asks her.

"No," she says in a whisper, palming her chest. Deja glances up to look at the face of the man that bumps into her. Her brows pressed together, seeing how sexy the man was with a head full of black, curly hair, trimmed mustache and goatee. He had broad shoulders and a big muscle build standing at least six feet two inches tall and probably weighing in at a solid two hundred pounds. *"You're a huge, sexy, Yeti man that almost knocked the dear life out of me! Damn!"* she wanted to say.

Deja's gaze was interrupted by the coldness of her white, work blouse touching her skin. They both looked down at her bosoms. "Mm mm, eyes up!" she tells the man, snapping back into reality and then tearing away from his hold.

"I'm sorry, miss," he says.

"No, it's my apologies."

"That looks like it's going to leave a stain there," he says.

"You think?" Deja sarcastically responds and then sighs. "Excuse me," she says, quickly turning away from him and going back into the restroom. There goes her work shift! Her evening couldn't get any worse after this.

Melissa, Deja's co-worker, comes into the bathroom, her dark brown hair flaring in the air. She was about to walk into a stall when she seen Deja at the mirror, repeatedly patting her shirt with a paper towel.

"Oh no, you had an accident?" Melissa says, walking over to Deja.

"I wasn't paying any attention," Deja's tone was obvious.

"Listen, I always carry a spare shirt just in case I end up with a wine spill on my shirt. My husband don't like it when I drink. You can borrow it if you can fit a size large," she generously offers Deja.

"Yea," Deja nods her head. "Thanks Melissa."

"No problem hun," she smiles and then continues into the stall.

With the help of Melissa, Deja was back on track again. Walking over to her next table to serve, she couldn't believe it when one of the guests was the man she bumped into; spotting him with a group of men. He still had a wet stain on his shirt from earlier.

"Welcome to the Hot Top, what can I get you gentlemen on this evening?" she asks them all, looking around at each of the four guys one at a time. After they gave their orders, Deja rushes away to turn it in to the cooks in the back.

Minutes later, serving their food, the man from earlier says, "You're the nicest waitress I ever ran across. Are you seeing someone?"

"I'm sorry, I'm on the clock right now. I can't answer that question," she plays it off.

"I'm Cavius, what's your name?" he asks her another question, a grin across his healthy pink lips.

"Deja," she quickly responds. Changing the subject, she asks them, "Is this all for you guys? Need anything else?"

"The answer to my first question. We're both grown right?" he says.

"First of all, there's a better way at approaching me during my line of work. You can do it the right way and wait until after I clock out. Complimenting me and asking me am I seeing someone afterwards, isn't it," she states, her eyes locked firmly on him.

Intrigued and suckling his teeth, Cavius says, "Is that right?"

"Yep, straight like that," she says to him.

"What time do you get off from work?" he asks her.

"I get off at 12," she says with a grin. This guy had a lot of nerve to holler at Deja while she's on the clock, but it makes him interesting to her.

"Okay, I'll see you afterwards then?" he returns a grin. Deja shrugs her shoulders and then walks away.

Tall and heavy bound, that man is too much man for Deja. She has a type and heavy weight, wrestling looking guys weren't it!

"Who's the handsome hunk of fellow out there?" Melissa teases her as they paired up together and cleaned the kitchen area.

"Who the Yeti guy?" Deja laughs.

"Yeti? Are you kidding me? He's a mountain that I would climb myself if I wasn't married!" Melissa jokes as they both share a laugh. "I never see you with a man. You should give him a try."

"Please, that man look like he'll flapjack me," Deja waves her hand and then starts washing the dishes. Melissa chuckles and says, "Girl, you better try him out first. My momma said you never know anything until you try it out." Melissa playfully nudges her elbow into Deja's arm, and then winks her eye.

"No way. I can't get to know a man right now. My son is getting out of pocket and my daughter is going through phases and stuff."

"Honey, sometimes you need a man to come into you and those kids' lives and take charge."

Take charge? Not over here! Hold the fuck up, Melissa! Only four out of five women commit to every man that comes into their lives, and Deja isn't four of them.

Commitment is a problem when it came down to her habits and these men getting in the way of them. With the urge to start robbing again and now that she's touched doped, Deja can relapse at any time. The money she made from both jobs were decent until there's hardly any leftover from paying the high ass light bill, rent and keeping up maintenance on her car.

"I'll think about it," Deja says. *Horny ass White woman... sometimes all they think about is riding big, Black dicks.* Deja don't need a man to take charge over anything she has going on with her life; she just needed a nigga to play his part and stay out of her business. Big Doug was all about that until he fucked her over on the rent money.

Walking out onto the lot, rather than the usual vehicles her coworkers drive, there was a silver Corvette on the lot as well. It was one of the new ones with a sleek model and those LED lights and pretty tail lights. Deja watches as a man emerges from the driver's seat with the height of nobody but Cavius.

She walks over to him, seeing that he didn't bother to leave and change out of his stained shirt from earlier. "So you really stayed huh?" she softly says.

"I'm a man of my word," he smiles from ear to ear. "I'd like to take you out sometime on your off day and get to know you," he says. "Or maybe even call you." Deja chuckles at the delighted thought of his words, if only they weren't so cliché.

"What's your number, Cavius?" she asks him, retrieving her phone from her purse. Deja hands her phone to him. After locking in his number, Cavius hands her the phone back. As she reaches for it, Cavius takes her hand with his free hand and brings it up to his mouth. He gently brushes his full, soft lips across the flat of her hand, and then says, "Your hands are so soft."

"I'm a woman, ain't I?" she jokes with him.

"Hey, some women skin be like alligators," he says, making her blush and giggle.

"Then you been messing with the wrong kind of women. I have to get going. You have my number, call me sometimes," she says to him and then walks away. Cavius lingers behind in his car until Deja drives off the lot; he doesn't trail after her.

Chapter 4

Finally an off day, Deja sat on the edge of the couch and laid back. With a half smoked backwoods in between her first and middle finger and the TV remote in the other one, she flipped through the channels finding something to watch when her cell phone vibrates beside her.

Deja glances over at the familiar number and answers, "Hello."

"Yo, Deja," said the voice of one of her old clients. She sat upright and then says, "Who is this?"

"This Chester," he replies.

"Aw, what's up," she sighs. Deja remembers Chester. He prefers bars and them new drugs than the old shit. He was her regular client, but he didn't do weed or powder.

"You got some of that Mary Jane, baby?" he asks her.

"Some weed? That ain't like you, Chester," she says.

"Well my nephew coming down from Indiana, and I ain't seen him in years. You got some for me?"

"Let me check and see and I'll call you right back," she says.

"Aight," he replies. They hang up at the same time.

Deja's eyes checked the front door to see if her son would walk through yet, which he didn't.

Somehow, getting back in the game just happened for Deja. She didn't want to take the time and go around from car to car or door to door like the old thief she was and steal stuff that hardly had no value these days. Drug money came fast for her, and it didn't come with Deja looking over her shoulder or running from a White butler with a shotgun like in Georgia.

After three rings, he picks up the phone and answers, "Hey, *mom deuce*."

"Don't call me that," she rolls her eyes as he loudly chuckles on the other end. "You got an ounce I can buy."

"Damn baby, you know I love a woman who knows what she's doing and what to do with some money. Why don't you deal for me?" Cane asks her.

"Cause that'll defeat the purpose of me not seeing your face all the time. Do you got an ounce, yes or no?"

"You know I got an ounce for you. Anything for you, *mom deuce*," he jokes with her again.

"I'll be over there in twelve minutes," she says.

"Hey, mom. I got a nice long, thirteen inches of -" *Click up!*

Deja hangs the phone up before he can finish. Cane can keep his ego and his long dick to himself, or whatever inches he's working with in his pants! She hardly wants to talk to Cavius, but Deja made an effort cause normally she'd pick a guy up in the club or somewhere.

Speaking of him, they had a date set for tonight on top of the Peabody hotel... real grown folks shit, she guessed.

Deja pulls on her clothes, gathers her purse and car keys and then leaves her duplex. She was straight to the business with Cane, getting her ounce of marijuana after giving him the money. Cane smiles to himself, seeing how

Deja opens the bag and then sniffles and checks out the weed, seeing that he really gave her kush.

"Don't I owe you extra?" she brings to his attention.

"Consider it a favor on hold from you when I need it," he then winks his eye at her, rubbing his hands together.

As soon as Deja left Cane's shotgun, trap house, she got back in contact with Chester. Even though something seems off about him, Deja made an effort to stash her ounce at the house inside of Rylee's teddy bear and then went to serve Chester.

He was stalling her, passing the time away for some apparent reason. Chester didn't even bother to offer his cash for the serve Deja had for him right away. *This shit is for the birds!*

Glancing down at the time, Deja seen that it's nearing the time for her to get ready for her date with Cavius. They had exchanged addresses and everything. She didn't need anything messing it up or her life at this moment.

"Aye, look. I have to go," Deja leans over to pull the door handle, as they sat inside Chester's old Buick car.

"Hey, wait a minute now! Where you going girl?" Chester grabs Deja by the other arm, yanking her back inside of the car.

"Get your motherfucking hands off me!" Deja yells at him, attempting to snatch her arm free.

"Now you know I don't smoke no weed baby! Come on now, I want something else," he says, his eyes trailing down to her pants.

Frowning, Deja growls at him, "You dirty old bitch!" Swinging first and losing her temper, Deja connected her right fist into Chester's face. She was amazed that the old man could take a punch, as it still didn't back him off her. She knew this was a bad idea!

"Come on now! Stop fighting!" Chester forcibly climbs

47

on top of Deja, restraining the arm he still had in his grip and locking her door with his free hand.

"No! I said get off me!" Deja shouts, feeling his cold hand tugging at the button of her pants. Breathing hard, filling with more rage, she really hates when a person doesn't listen to her, and she had to get herself out this situation. Whether Chester is stronger than her or not, Deja was gonna give him the best she got.

She leans forward and bites her teeth into Chester's nose, not caring if she tasted snot or his boogers along the way. He screams aloud, trying to pull free from her. Chester takes his hands and wraps them around Deja's neck as she now felt her phone vibrating in her pocket.

"You wanna fight me huh! It's more than one way to skin a pussycat!" he cackles, his eyes filling with excitement.

She would've rolled down the window and waved her hand out in the open if there was a car to pass down the road, but they were parked on an abandoned dead end street.

Deja couldn't panic or give in right away. Feeling for the cigarette burner from the dashboard, Deja plucks it out and then connects it to Chester's eye. He hollers out again, and then angrily punches her in the mouth. It hurt like hell for Deja to feel her lip burst into a wound, later followed by the taste of blood in her mouth.

Before he could get close on her, as Chester held his eye, still mounted on top of Deja and loudly screaming in her face, Deja takes her hand and whacks Chester into his throat, knocking the air out of him. He falls off of her and back into the driver's seat, gasping for air and holding his neck with both hands.

"You old sick, fuck!" she then spits on him and unlocks the door, hopping out of the car. Chester was unable to talk shit to Deja before she runs off.

With her phone vibrating in her pocket again, Deja takes it out, seeing that it was Cavius calling. "Shit!" she hisses, tucking the phone away and into her pocket. There goes her planned date, ruined and over with.

When Deja made it to the sidewalk of her house, she should've known to see Cavius's little silver Corvette car parked behind hers. She couldn't embarrass herself like this; beat up because some old man wanted her pussy and not weed that she had planned on selling to him.

Her phone went vibrating again as Deja took a moment and hid on the side of her neighbor's tree. Pulling herself together, she answers, "Hello?"

"Hey, I was wondering is you still up for tonight? I'm in your driveway," he says.

Watching him from around the tree, Deja replies back, "Oh, I done messed around and caught a bug one of these kids brought through the door from school."

"Really? Well do you need anything from the store?" he asks her, sounding generous and soft. That's not the type of guy she needs. Deja know for a fact now he wouldn't be the type of man that'll be okay with her lifestyle. He won't do his part and stay out of her business. It's a no for her on *them*.

"I'm straight. I mean, I already have unsalted crackers and chicken noodle soup here from when my baby girl got sick. I'm good," she lies, briefly coughing; it wasn't a fake cough, her throat was still agitated from nearly being choked out.

"Okay, I guess I'll catch up to you later," he says.

"Yea, I'll text you when I'm better."

"Okay, goodnight Deja."

"Night, Cavius," she says, hurting her lip to smile.

Sore with a busted, and swollen lip, Deja watches as Cavius backs up out the driveway and then leaves, his car disappearing down the street. She rushes over to her duplex and then unlocks the door, finding her kids all the in the living room watching TV. The lights were on and the smell of hot wings and rotel came from the kitchen.

Pausing, her eyes were on them as their eyes were all on her.

"Oh my gosh, mom! What the hell happened to you!" Raine gets up from the couch, cuffing her hand over her mouth.

Marterrio races over to Deja, frowning, strongly resembling an image of his dad. "Who did this to you?" he asks her.

"I'm fine," she says, brushing him off her. Deja walks past them all and into the hallway.

She didn't feel like being bothered with, locking her bedroom door and falling down across the bed. Deja wasn't fine; even though there was no loss, she felt like Chester still had to pay for what he did.

With her oldest kids not speaking to her, Deja even avoided Cavius until her mouth healed. Chester had the nerve to call and send harassing threats to her phone, and she'd block his number. She let the kids go to Georgia to spend time with their dads while she attempted to make things right with Cavius. He's soft... but his looks and height were everything in a man she could ask for.

When she first found out about Cavius address, Deja googled it right away to see that he lived downtown in one of those houses on the riverfront. She didn't bother going until now.

With a bottle of Crown Royal in one hand and a home cooked meal in the other, Deja had walked up to back garage door, wearing her best and new attire. She had her hair down in ripples of curls with not that much jewelry or make-up on.

50

Before she could gently knock on the door with her knuckles, the door handle moves downward and the door is pulled open. Wearing a Versace shirt and a pair of black dress pants, Cavius answers the door and smiles.

"Well, look at who the crisp weather blew over," he says with a grin. Cavius checks her out from head to toe and then invites Deja inside. "Has anyone told you that you look beautiful with your hair down like that before?" he compliments her as she follows him from the small laundry area and right into the kitchen.

"I barely wear my hair down so I wouldn't know. How have you been?" she asks him, nervous and growing horny at the same time. Maybe that's why she's really attracted to him. The words that Melissa said got in her head. *"Climb that mountain!"* Maybe he can bounce her up and down on the dick while in the air? *What if his dick is little though? Probably not happening!*

"I been alright. Working, and thinking about you," he replies as they reach the kitchen.

"This is nice," Deja says, marveling his kitchen and how neatly it's cleaned and organized as if a woman lives with him. "Looks almost like a woman lives here."

"Men can't be organized too?" he asks her.

"I haven't met a guy that was."

"Well you met the right one, baby," he says. *Baby?* Deja had almost cringed at that word, which she now slightly disliked. Noticing the change in her mood, Cavius asks her, "Did I say something wrong?"

"I'm not big on the word 'baby'," she admits and then gently sighs.

"My apologies," he says. Leaning on the center counter island, Deja watches as Cavius turns his back to her to fix them both a glass of ice. The folds of his shirt hugging the muscles in his back and arms every now and then when he would reach for something. *What a man, what a man, what a mighty sexy man?*

"I know this is silly of me asking but do you work out a lot or, you know… take protein shakes?" she asks him, curious to know these things, her stomach fluttering with curiosity. Deja never ran across a big and tall, strong man with Cavius's physique before.

Chuckling as he turns around with their shot glasses of ice, Cavius answers, "No, I don't drink protein shakes, and I was just born healthy. I take after my dad. He's six feet four inches tall with a strong body build."

"Wow, so do you have to eat like full course meals or you're not picky? I mean, cause I cooked, but -"

Smiling from the corner of his lips, Cavius then says, "Relax, I love a home cooked meal, and I'm not a big eater. What about you? Where the kids at?"

"With their dads," she replies. Deja intensely watches him as he first pours lemonade in both of their glasses, adding Mango rum and then the Crown Royal she brought over. *He knows how to fix drinks, that's a plus.*

One time Deja had asked Big Doug to make her a drink and that nigga tried to drown her liver in one sip. Deja couldn't halfway get the liquor down her throat without choking.

"More than one?" he asks her.

"Well, my oldest son have his dad to himself and my two girls have the same father."

"So you're entirely free for this holiday weekend?" Cavius walks around the counter island and up to Deja, offering her drink.

"Some like that. I'm not free from working," she says and chuckles, breaking eye contact from his bright brown eyes. Deja takes a sip from her drink, taking in the alcoholic fruity flavor; Cavius does the same. She had took another big sip so fast and pulled away, Deja was startled when Cavius reaches for her lips and then gently smooths his thumb over the corner of her bottom lip, saying in a soft voice, "I got it." He gently wipes away the leftover alcohol.

Clearing her throat, Deja steps back from Cavius and says, "Well, so what do you have in mind to do huh? I'm not off again until Wednesday."

"I did want to take you out on the town and see a play then go shopping and stuff," he says.

"A play?" Deja's brows presses together.

"You think Black people don't like to see broadways plays too?" he asks her, they both chuckle.

"I mean, I haven't before. It'll be something new to me," she says.

"Come on, let me show you the rest of the house," he says, walking away.

They settled into the cozy den that overlooked the sweeping views of the Mississippi River and all its glory. Cavius assisted Deja in removing her jacket and hangs in on an elegant coat hanger nearby. She was intrigued by the interior designs and home décor arranged on the surrounding walls. There had to be a woman living here on the low.

"So, you know where I work at. What do you do for a living?" Deja asks him, almost finished with her drink. Sitting in chill mode with his arm outstretched along the couch behind Deja, Cavius was already done with his glass.

"I own an entertainment club with three different locations across the board and some stock for Samsung. I also have a small business front that deals with affordable life insurance," he replies with a smile and a straight face. Deja wouldn't be convinced if he didn't look her in the eyes, but liars do that too.

"Oh," she says, amazed with his answer. "Really though? So you're like a boss, huh? That's how you can afford this?"

"Well, it's only me. Even though I do have a kid on the way," he shrugs his shoulders.

"Oh," Deja sings, covering her mouth with her hand, shocked and disappointed. To keep her face from frowning, Deja clears her throat and looks away.

Okay, he's probably three or four years older than Deja, which also means that he could be fertile. She can't make things serious between them.

"Is that a bad thing?" he asks her.

"No," she forces a smile, "just a congratulations. Is it your first?"

"I have a child out of state," he says with a blank face, his sturdy eyes on hers. Cavius watches for Deja's shocked expression that she couldn't hide. He then laughs and says, "Nah! I'm just joking. I'm just fucking with ya. I only have one on the way."

Hehehe, I should boop boop your ass, motherfucker! Deja deeply exhales and nervously chuckles; she still didn't catch the joke.

"She's not the one for me though. I mean...she's having my baby but she don't have my heart," he says, and then looks away.

"Yea, it be that way sometimes. I don't think I am neither," she says, flattering herself. Cavius turns to face Deja again, locking her gaze in his eyes.

"Really?"

"Yep, I'm a baddie," she jokes with him. Cavius grins from ear to ear, gravity pulling them into each other's atmospheres. They were so close that they could smell the alcohol on each other's breath.

"You're a baddie? How bad?" Cavius asks her. Deja

sets down her glass onto the floor and then says, "Very bad."

Irresistible to his gaze as their eyes continuing to lock onto each other, Deja makes her move first, leading the way as Cavius follows. Cavius's hands holds onto Deja's waist as she climbs on top of him. Kissing him slow and passionate, her soft and moist lips moving against his, as Deja rubs her hands over his chiseled chest.

She wasn't just pleasing him, but checking for muscles in his broad chest that was present. Deja felt one muscle at a time. *"Climb that mountain!"* Melissa's voice says in her head.

Deja pulls away from him, parting her lips to say something when Cavius strongly pulls her back close to him; she felt his harness through his pants. *Oh, he's ready ready!* Drunk and giggling, Deja was amazed as Cavius lifts up from the couch seat with Deja in one arm and then lays her down onto the couch.

She undid her clothes as Cavius did the same, the both of them tossing their clothes in the air not caring where it lands. With just her bra and panties on, Cavius takes the tip of his tongue between her chest, nibbling on the meat of her breasts. He takes his hands along the outmost of her thighs, lightly tracing his fingers against her flesh, sending chills up Deja's spine.

It was too early to fuck, but the moment and setting felt so right. Fully undressed, Deja firmly sits on top of Cavius, pushing him inside her moist pussy. She gently moans, shutting her eyes and turning her head away. The last guy was just thick and average, but Deja couldn't say the same for Cavius.

Normally, she'd fuck, but this evening Deja had her mind on making love to Cavius... for one evening only. With her feet firmly planted on the side of Cavius thighs,

Deja slowly grinds her hips in a circular, up and down motion. He reaches behind her, rubbing his hands around her ass cheeks.

"Mm, just like that," Cavius groans. Deja takes his hands from behind her, biting her lips and then places his big hands over her full breasts. She caught a steady rhythm, grinding her hips more and penetrating him inside of her deeper, in full control of Cavius's long, fourteen-inch dick.

"Oh my god," she moans, leaning over him, her body feeling intense and her toes curling. Deja bounces her hips up and down atop of Cavius, his shaft stroking her g-spot. He takes his hand and slaps her ass, and then rests them behind his head, watching Deja dominate him.

Getting up onto her feet, balancing herself, Deja bounced harder on him, planting her hand in the middle of his firm chest. She momentarily glances down at the two of them, seeing her pussy cream all over Cavius's dick. She could fell him throbbing inside of her, returning back to grinding on her knees on top of him.

"Shit! Fuucck! Do that shit then!" Cavius says, slapping Deja on the ass again. "Let me get up," he later says in a near moan.

Deja didn't want to let up, staying in control, she rode him faster. Hearing Cavius's toe knuckles popping after the other, Deja held on tight as he now starts pounding her from underneath. Cavius wraps his arms around her waist, holding her steady to him, pounding her wet pussy, the sound of his thighs slapping against her thighs.

"Oh! Oh! Oooohh sshiiit! Cavius!" Deja loudly screams his name in ecstasy, gripping her breasts in both hands. Taking her by surprise, Cavius had moved her off him. No longer in control, Deja assumes the position, her ass high in the air and arching her back. Deja reaches behind her and spreads her cheeks apart for him.

Taking the length of her hair in his hands, he tightly wounds Deja's hair around his wrist and then slides his dick into her wet pussy. As she loudly moans out, Cavius tugs onto her hair and says, "You gone take it?"

"Yes," she answers him.

"Back that ass up then," he says and then releases her hair.

Moaning with every deep stroke, Deja could feel him pulsating again inside of her. "Look back at me," he orders her in a low tone. Deja obediently glances back at Cavius, still sliding back and forth on his dick. Their moans were accompanied with the sounds of a sticky noise. Cavius' eyes roll to the back of his head and he holds his head up to the ceiling. Deja looks away, sliding back and forth harder, *fucking him back.*

Cavius takes her hair around his fists and roughly starts pounding her, his balls loudly smacking against the back of her thighs. Deja grabs the sheets, holding on tight.

"Ah! Aaahhh!" Cavius loudly groans.

"Sshhiiit!" Deja hisses, coming with him.

"Mm," Cavius moans, still going in and out of Deja, her pussy dripping wet, its juices running out of her.

Both panting and catching their breaths, Cavius rests on the side of Deja with his eyes closed. Deja rolls onto her side and props herself up onto her elbow, checking him out. She didn't think he'd fall asleep that fast until she heard him briefly snoring with his mouth open.

After handling her hygiene, Deja pulls on her clothes and leaves before Cavius could wake up. She should expect for him to be calling, but Deja didn't plan on answering.

She couldn't wait to get back to her second job to brag

to Melissa and tell her about it. They were assigned to clean the dining area.

"Well, aren't you just golly and glowing?" Melissa says, approaching Deja first, who smiles to herself. "Somebody must've had a date with the Mountain?" Melissa jokes with Deja.

"Yes and it will be a hit and run," Deja grins from ear to ear. "That man gave me the whole lightening show without holding back."

Melissa gasps, and her eyes grew wide with excitement as she says, "Did you climb the mountain?"

"I climbed and conquered it," Deja says, the two of them laughing out loud and locking their high five.

"How was he? Like his girth size?" Melissa curiously asks. The two of them had now stopped working to talk.

"Long, thick and juicy. If we didn't get straight to the point, I believed I would've did my best to suck the soul right out of him," Deja giggles.

"Oh," Melissa coos. "And how about he claims that he's an entrepreneur and owns a lot of this and that to afford living a comfortable lifestyle right up there off Front Street?"

"No way! My brother-in-law lives that way. Those places are expensive for the river views, but they're hell of nice," Melissa palms her chest.

"Can you believe it though?"

"Yes, I can," Melissa says. "A lot of Black men are well off just as the White ones, hun. You better hook and reel that one in, Deja."

"I don't know. He has a child on the way," she shrugs her shoulders and then glances past Melissa to see their manager walk by. Even though he didn't walk out into the dining room, they return to working.

"And what does that supposed to mean? As long as it's

just one, right?" Melissa shrugs her shoulders. "My husband had a two year old baby while mine was only one at the time when we got married. Honey bee, you think I cared? No hun, I went on and married my husband, and we been nine years going strong now," Melissa shakes out the trash of her towel over the rolling, trash bin.

Deja had every intention towards blocking Cavius's number and enjoying her free time alone. She'd go into her first job, work two extra hours and go in early to her second job, also keeping up with her work hours.

Now clocking out of work, there was a black BMW coupe, parked on the side of her car. Deja looks across the lot to see Melissa happily hopping into her husband's pick-up truck; the others had already left.

Nearing her car, Deja clutches her fists until a familiar, strong body build, tall figure exits the driver's side. Squinting her eyes and walking faster, Deja calls out, "Cavius? What are you doing here?"

"I been calling you for four days now," he states, his voice calm. "What's wrong? You don't like me? Was my sex too much for you?"

"Really?" she gasps in a chuckle. "I mean, the other night was on point. I just want to enjoy the rest of my week away from the kids."

"But you're counting me out in the process. You seeing someone else or something?"

"Wait, hold on. It's really late, and I don't feel like talking about this right now."

Cavius grabs Deja by the arm, and repeats himself, "You seeing someone else or something?"

"No, I'm not," Deja honestly answers him. Cavius deeply sighs, tilting his head to the side.

"Why don't you come over?" he says without releasing her arm.

"Tonight?" her brows presses together.

"Yea."

"I – I have work tomorrow morning. I can't," she says.

"I won't hold you up, I promise," he says. "Can I just have an hour of your time tonight?"

Deja swallows hard and says, "Okay, Cavius."

After getting into their separate cars, Deja trails behind Cavius to his condo on Front Street. She hadn't even had the time from her first job to shower and take a nap.

Deja now felt uneasy around Cavius, thinking that he just wants to fuck. Leaving her purse behind in the foyer, she trails after Cavius and into the den... where it all started with the two of them.

Like the gentlemen he is, Cavius removes her jacket and places it on the coat rack nearby. Deja takes a seat on the small loveseat couch, seeing that nothing was arranged different or misplaced from the last time she came over.

"Is you hungry or want something to drink?" he asks Deja, standing near the doorway that lead into a different hallway.

"Um, just probably something light to drink."

"You should try my frozen, wine slush with rum," he suggests and then walks away before Deja could turn down his offer.

Deja hadn't planned on getting comfortable, even though she wanted to. She gets up from the couch and takes a walk around the room, noticing Cavius's pictures. He even had plaques on the wall of his achievements, pictures captured of where he's been in the world. Cavius was even part of a motorcycle club; it's all too real to be true. There had to be more to him than what she's seeing.

Minutes later, Cavius returns with a wine glass in each hand, filled with a cold beverage. He joins Deja on the couch and then sets his glass down on the table after giving Deja her glass.

"Thanks," she softly says.

"How was work?" Cavius asks her, lowering himself down to her feet. Deja glares at him aside his head and then quickly scoots her feet back.

"What are you doing?" she asks him, nearly frowning.

"Calm down, Deja. I'm only removing your shoes," he calmly says. Reaching forward, Deja moves her feet to the right side of her and away from him.

"Look, I really had a long day of work at both jobs. Unlike you and other successful people out here, I don't have passive income. I have to clock in and out of work almost every day," she fumes as Cavius now leans over and places his finger against her lips.

"Sh! I understand," he says.

"You do?" Deja wasn't reassured, giving him that look.

"Yea, you're a single mother and a hard working woman that's providing for her family. You're a grown ass woman out here. So, let me take this hour and dedicate it to you. Just relax, Deja," Cavius returns to kneeling down before Deja. She watches in awe as he removes one shoe after the other, later massaging her feet and toes. Deja deeply exhales, relaxing and taking a sip of her frozen, wine slush. It's popping fruity flavor and rum danced along her taste buds. *She ain't never had it like this before!*

After massaging her feet for five minutes, Cavius stands up and then says, "Stay here. I'll be back with something to snack on." Deja quickly glances at the time, seeing that it's almost one in the morning.

"Cavius?" she calls after him, but he walks away. Deja sighs and her eyes look at the time on her phone again.

Playing it nice, Deja waits until Cavius returns with a

silver tray filled with a variety of diced and cut fruit, garnished with large green leaves.

"Oh wow," Deja coos, amazed at Cavius and his behavior. *He must want the neck tonight!* Deja now forces a smile, shaking away her sexual thoughts. This is not what she intended to be over here for.

"I ran you a warm, salt bath by the way, if that's okay?"

"I can't spend the night, Cavius. My work clothes is at my place," she sighs.

"You worry too much," he says, and then takes Deja by the hand. "I could actually take care of you and the kids if you let me."

"I'm so used to doing it by myself," Deja nervously chuckles. "You must forgot when I said I'm bad."

"I don't think you have a bad bone in your body. You're probably naughty, but not bad. I've met bad women before and they were bad off in their mind," Cavius says, guiding Deja down the dim lit hallway, her hand in one of his hands and the fruit platter in the other. The corridor ended at a pair of double metal doors. Cavius opens one of them and they enter, walking into a large bedroom that had its own sitting area.

Deja could smell cinnamon apple scented candles, a small fireplace to the left of the room was lit and there were tall candlelit poles in random spots around the room. "Well aren't you romantic?" Deja says, playing it hard. Cavius grins and then guides her from the bedroom and into the bathroom where a large, built in tub filled with bubble bath and a bath pillow near the rim of the tub waited for her.

"Clothes off," he orders her with a grin.

Deja returns a smile and says, "Only if you'll join me."

It wasn't her intention to be body to body with Cavius

in his big tub, kissing on him like two White people in a movie with his arms holding her tight to him. Deja couldn't resist him at this point.

"Okay, okay! It's getting late and I really gotta go," she says, pulling away from him.

"Come here," Cavius calmly says, staring her in the eyes. As Deja was hesitant, he swims over to her, his hand going down her hip, between her thighs. Cavius holds Deja close to him, suckling and kissing on her neck with his fingers massaging her clitoris.

"Ooohh," Deja moans and then gently bites down onto Cavius's strong shoulder, later kissing the same spot. "Wait, wait! I'm too tired to... you know. It's not what I had in mind," Deja moans.

"Say you want me to stop then," Cavius says into her ear, his voice melting down her earlobe, his finger moving faster. Unable to speak, feeling her stomach cave in, Deja holds onto the edge of the tub with one hand and Cavius neck with her other arm.

"Cavius..." she exhales, trying her best to keep from coming.

"Mmm," he moans into her ear.

Climaxing and coming at the same time, multiple moans release from Deja's mouth before she loudly groans out, "Ooohhh!" Leaning over onto him, her pelvic shivers as Cavius gently strokes her clit afterwards.

"You might want to call in right now and tell your supervisor you won't be making it in," Cavius says into her ear. Deja giggles in agreement, officially ready to lay down to sleep.

Deja normally likes to do all the work, but she's too tired to even fuck. Like a winged spread eagle, Deja laid stretched out across the bed in pure ecstasy, her pussy juices being sucked and slurped up by Cavius. She had climaxed at least four times over; she could've sworn that she had no more pussy left for Cavius to eat and nibble after the fourth climax.

The following morning, Deja didn't care to call into her job after being ate out all night long. She cared enough about her sleep, and Cavius didn't bother to wake her up. His bed was big and comfortable, and soft. She didn't mind the warmth of being held that Cavius provided during her sleep. And Deja felt the big difference of when he was gone; it gave her the notion that what they had going on isn't playing out.

After waking up, Deja rinsed off the soft musk odor from her sleep and then pulls on one of Cavius's huge tee shirts, its tail hovering past her thighs like a dress. Deja takes her fingers and combs her long hair around to the other side of her neck. Stomach growling, she exits the bedroom and then went down the same hall she did last night, one of the exits leading into the kitchen.

Upon entering the kitchen, she hears a guy loudly cackles, sounding like his laugh came right from his stomach, nearly startling Deja. She stops walking at first to make sure if what she was hearing is right; Cavius has company.

"So I'm just like Junior, if you gone clock a nigga, at least hit him in the side of his head in the front!" the other guy says, his voice matching the tone of Cavius's. "Lil Junior had slapped the nigga," he later adds, the two of them sharing a laugh again, their voice identical to each other. Deja's brows presses together in confusion.

"So how are we looking like at the shop?"

"Ten thousand worth of ice came in last night and there's more to come again, same time," the other guy says. *Ice?! This nigga runs an ice shop! What the fuck?*

"It's the hottest thing out now," a familiar voice now

chimes in. Deja felt her head briefly sway to the side as she almost lost her balance.

"Aye man, let me grab some to drink right fast," said the familiar voice. Startled, Deja's eyes grew wide as they drop down to what she's wearing, now feeling uncomfortable and out of place. Light on her feet, she flees from the kitchen, damn near bumping her shoulder into the doorway right before Cavius's guest walks in.

"Seen you got a car outside? Looks like somebody I know of," his voice says, sounding closer like he wasn't across the kitchen. Deja would've crept down the hall if she wasn't interesting in eavesdropping on Cavius and his guests' conversation. Who were those guys? One sounds like Cavius and the other sounds like the Cane nigga?

"You think you know every woman in Memphis," Cavius now says from the kitchen with his deep voice.

"Only if their a milf," the guy chuckles.

"Whatever, I'll be right back," Cavius says.

Oh shit! Deja rushes down the hall towards the bedroom and swiftly turns around. Pretending like she's just now leaving his room, Deja clears her throat and forces a smile, encountering Cavius.

"Well good morning," Cavius smiles from ear to ear and wounds his arms around Deja. Embracing her, Cavius pecks his lips onto her forehead.

"Mm, morning," Deja says in return, and they pull away from each other.

"I think you wear this better than me," he says, checking her out in his shirt.

"You think so?" Deja seductively lifts and pulls at the shirt tail.

"I'm feeling it," he takes his hand behind her and grabs a handful of her ass, making Deja blush. "There's two knuckle heads I want you to meet," he later says.

"Now? So soon?" she asks him, looking confused.

"Chill out; they're only my brothers," he says.

"Yea... I um, gotta go. I already missed my work shift and I have to make a few errands and stuff," she says to him, scratching the back of her head. "I mean... maybe some other time." She did want to find out who the hell Cavius had in the living room, but she didn't. The truth might scare the hell out of her.

"Okay?" Cavius raises his brows. Lifting his hands in the air as if he's surrendering, Cavius turns on his heels and walks away without saying anything else. Deja sighs, holding up the length of her hair into her hands.

Returning to the bedroom, Deja pulls on her pants from last night, stuffing her work shirt, bra and panties down into her purse to spare herself the embarrassment. Leaving her hair down, Deja finally makes her way to the living room where there was only Cavius left. She could hear the sounds of car engines revving to life on the outside.

"I'm gone, Cavius," she says to him.

"See you around," Cavius responds with his back facing her. Deja showed herself out the door and to her car, seeing that one of the vehicles still lingered behind with dark tinted windows and windshield in one of those new vehicles.

She could play the waiting game, but Deja left first.

Chapter 5

During her sleep, Deja could hear her cell phone loudly ringing on the side of her. She peeped her eyes open and glances past her. Resting on the outer side of her pillow, near the edge of the bed, Deja's phone screen gently illuminated her room. She reaches over and picks it up, seeing that it was Cavius's number.

Deja checks the time, seeing that it's seven in the morning; maybe this man has no life? Sighing, she waits to see if he'll call back after not answering the phone. To her surprise, he didn't. Thinking it's over, Deja was just about to shut her eyes close when she hears an alarming car horn, loudly blaring from the outside.

"What the hell?" Deja snatches the cover off from over her and hops out of bed. As she makes it to the door, the horn stops.

Deja barges out from her duplex and up to Cavius's car; he rolls the window down and grins at her. "Good morning, I hope you like breakfast muffins?" he says. *Nigga, what the hell?*

Astounded and amazed at the same time, Deja folds

her arm across her breasts and says, "What the hell is your problem?"

"I figured that you wasn't going to answer the phone when I called, so here we are. Just because we had a small disagreement, it doesn't mean that I'm upset at you," he says.

"Do you know what time it is? I have work in like another hour. I'm not calling in to my job for a fourth time. They're going to fire me," she rants and then exhales.

"Well then we'll have breakfast in your place. I'll be inside in a minute," he says and rolls the window up. Deja remains standing with her arms folded, amazed at Cavius's response and his actions. Any other guy doing this would have Deja messed up, but not him. It's a good thing she cleaned up last night before work.

"My place isn't as fancy or decorated as yours," Deja now says on their way up to the front door. She helps Cavius with his load of food that he had cooked and brought along.

"I didn't always have my flat on Front Street." He follows behind Deja as they enter into her small duplex.

"That's interesting, I guess," she says. "I'll be back. I have to freshen up." Before Cavius could stop her, she was already in the hallway.

Deja quickly handled her hygiene in the bathroom, combing her hair up into a ponytail and then joining Cavius in the small eating area. He had the table set and ready for them.

"So, have you ever considered going into business for yourself or going to college?" he asks her.

"Nope," Deja bluntly says, her morning with him already getting stale. Cavius had cooked from his home and brought to hers, breakfast muffins made out of eggs, sausage, cheese and chives, bacon, grits and toast. Deja's mind never thought big of college. It didn't excite her; having a hustle did more than getting a degree.

"What if you could own your morning job?" he asks her from across the table. Deja blankly looks at him, not touching her food.

"Really? A cleaning company?"

"Or what if you could own your own cleaning company?"

"I don't like cleaning after people and they shit," she bluntly says and then starts eating.

"The whole reason of me asking is because I grew up seeing both of my parents working two jobs to get me and my brothers out the ghetto and made sure that we stayed that way. My mom went to school to be a Registered Nurse and graduated at the age of fifty," he explains.

"That's nice to know," she says, continuing to eat her food.

The hour had went by so fast, as soon as Deja was done eating, she had quickly pulled on her work clothes. On their way out, Cavius stops Deja at the door and they turn to face each other.

Taking his arm around her waist and pulling her close to him, Cavius says to Deja, "You know one of these days, when you're ready to let go and not be afraid to be with me, you won't have to worry about calling in to work or going to make your next paycheck. I'll have you waking up getting ready for your spa appointment and then brunch while the nanny tend to the kids."

Delighted at his thought, Deja giggles and then blushes. She pulls away from him, and prattles, "Although that does sounds nice, I have two teenagers and a five-year-old."

"One day you'll see," he then leans in to kiss her on the forehead.

It would be nice for Deja to wake up without the weight of the world on her shoulders. She passed up a good opportunity with Reese, letting another woman get the ring. Cavius is soft like Reese, but he has more money.

Now cleaning the kitchen as they were assigned to, Melissa was in the pantry taking a cup of wine to the head. "I just love this brand," Melissa says, holding one the restaurant's expensive bottles on the menu in her dainty hand. "Wanna cup?" she offers Deja.

"Why not?" Deja says, closing the pantry door behind her. Deja grabs a glass and pours herself a cup, and they toast their glasses.

"I can't get enough and it's like my husband knows it," she says.

"There's nothing wrong with drinking to be merry," Deja concurs. "This is the last day until my kids come back home tomorrow. I've had one hell of a week with Cavius."

"Ooh," Melissa playfully nudges Deja in the arm. "So did y'all go on a little rendezvous?"

"No, not really. But we had a small bump along the way the other day. I didn't want to meet his brothers cause one of them sounded like someone I knew from the past. I left and didn't contact him and just this morning he's calling my phone. I don't answer and then he blows his horn from the driveway. We have breakfast and he asks me weird questions -"

"Like what?" Melissa cuts her off with a grin.

"He asked me do I think of owning my own business or going back to college. I am straight up out of the gutter. I've never looked forward to going to college...ever!"

Melissa's cheeks lit with color and she chuckles at Deja. "I absolutely agree with you. My husband has a Bachelors in IT and look at us? My sister's husband has a better living than us and he has a trade."

"So he goes on about taking care of me one day. It sounded nice and all, but I have a teenage son and daughter. I don't think they'll like him."

"Honey, there's nothing wrong with respecting your kids and your home, but that man can do things for you that your kids can't!" Melissa says in the most honest way. "If I was you, I would move my way into that man's world and heart. Look at him. He's tall, hunky, and has long money," she imitates the movement of her hands as if she's throwing money, making Deja laugh.

"You know what? You know what? If I wasn't married to my husband and a guy like Cavius comes around to change my life and he's bonafide... honey, I would be all over that. Men like Mountain Cavius only come a dime a dozen," Melissa then takes a large gulp from her glass, finishing the rest of her wine. Deja couldn't agree with Melissa cause her thoughts weren't sober right now. It's hard for Deja to let men in when she's the way that she is.

"You think so?"

"Yes!" Melissa exclaims. "Quit being so anti and get to know the man for Christ's sakes."

On her way out, Deja receives a text from Marterrio stating that they're all back at the house, and his dad is there. She was glad that Cavius wasn't hounding around her like he was the other night.

Deja made it to the house quicker than her usual drive time. Parked in the driveway in her spot was a black Dodge Charger.

As soon as she walks through the front door, Jayceon was in the living room, sitting on her couch with the TV on. There's something about seeing a man in the front of a TV that Deja dislikes.

Marterrio emerges from the kitchen with a bowl of cereal, abruptly stopping when he sees his mom. "Boy, you know not to be eating in my living room!" she fumes at him.

"It's for me," Jayceon says.

Deja closes her front door shut and says, "Do you know what time it is? What is you doing here so late? Scratch that, what are you doing here at all?"

"My son sleeps on your couch here, Deja. He's about to be eighteen. Don't you think it's time for him to come and live with me?"

Deja glances aside Jayceon's head and then her eyes went to glare at Marterrio, who continues to give his dad the bowl of cereal. Walking over, Deja takes the bowl right out of Marterrio's hands in midair during passing it, and then says, "The rules still applies. You could've at least waited until tomorrow evening and found you a motel room!"

"What's with the static? You afraid your little boyfriend gonna feel some type of way or some?" Jayceon says with a wicked smile on his face.

Deja's brows pushes together and she says, "He's too real to blow up over a man he has no competition with."

"You think so?" Jayceon sits back onto the couch.

"I know so," Deja walks away with the bowl of cereal. Jayceon gets up from the couch and follows behind her.

"So you mad?" he asks from behind her.

"I'm not mad. It's the principle of respect, Jay. I work all the time and Marterrio knows this. So instead of him telling you, being the child that he is-" Deja now yells from the kitchen, directing it towards Marterrio. She returns her attention back to Jayceon and says, "-you could've planned to tell me something like this! This could've waited until tomorrow."

"Let me ask you some? Is you serious with this man? I thought Reese could hold your lil bad ass down, but he

72

couldn't. I assumed that Big Doug was just someone for long term, but that went down south -"

Deja cuts him off, "Hey, you can't go talking about my past relationships like that."

"Are you serious with this guy or not, I'm asking you to make sure. Whoever he is has you in an uproar about the thought of me being over," Jayceon grins again, leaning in closer to Deja.

"Nothing personal Jayceon, but our time been over with. I'm not serious with this guy. I think he's too good for me," she admits, looking him in the eyes.

"You're thinking that, but deep down inside, you don't really know that," he says in a low voice. Both of them were nodding their heads in agreement, until Deja breaks away.

The two of them sit at the table; Deja slides the bowl of cereal across its wooden surface to Jayceon. He catches it and starts eating, and then says with a mouthful of cereal, "You didn't let me in, Reese in or other niggas. What's the real matter with you, Deja?"

Without looking at him and leaning onto her elbow, Deja shrugs her shoulders. She's tired from work, that's all she knows.

"Bring your guard down sometimes. It doesn't hurt to let someone in," he says.

"Look, I'm really tired. So, you're allowed this one night only over here, alright?" she then stands up from the table. Jayceon continues to eat his cereal as Deja exits the kitchen.

Deja had showered, locked her bedroom door and then drifted off into a deep sleep as soon as she hit the bed.

Unlike majority of the guys she's dated, only Jayceon knew of her wild side...the real Deja. He knew how she couldn't keep her hands to herself or away from nice things she wanted. Jayceon knew of Deja's demons and her struggle to not go back to her old lifestyle.

To let Cavius into her world was like exposing herself. Deja's only concern was having Cavius being able to handle the truth.

The girls are familiar with Jayceon as he is with them. Like the man he is, he moves Deja's car out of the way and uses his car instead to take the girls to school, leaving Marterrio at the house.

Sleeping past her alarm, Deja awakes at last minute from her sleep. She gets out of bed and goes from her room and into the girls, seeing them gone. Deja encounters Marterrio in the hallway as she turns around. "My dad took the girls to school ten minutes ago," he softly says.

Deja sighs in relief and then returns to her bedroom without another word. Still sleepy, she handles her hygiene, letting her hair hang down for once today since the weather isn't so hot outside. Finished and rejuvenated, Deja goes into the kitchen and cooks up something small.

Jayceon arrives twenty minutes later and joins her in the kitchen. With his car keys in his hand, he sits at the table, marveling the length of Deja's hair; she rarely wears her hair down, and when she does you can't help but stare.

"So, miss lady, about our conversation from last night," he says.

Now able to think, Deja's mind is more clear than last night. Fixing herself a cup of coffee with cream and sugar, Deja sits at the table and then firmly says, "Get in here, Marterrio."

Taking a few sips from the warm rim of the mug, the hot liquid flowing down her throat, Deja waits for Marterrio to come into the kitchen. He stands on the side of the table with his dad.

"Did your son tell you that he has a court date coming in another two days?" she asks Jayceon.

"He told me he had a run-in with the law," he says in a low tone.

"I'm lucky his case isn't criminal but it's downstairs in general court sessions," Deja takes two more sips of her coffee before placing the mug down. "Instead of taking him away from me, why don't you move back to Memphis. That way, he'll have both of his parents close."

"That does sound good, but I made a life for myself in the A," Jayceon says. "Maybe we can work something out where he'll spend a summer over."

"When I turn 18, I'm moving in with you," Marterrio says, deciding for himself. Irritated, Deja eyes Marterrio and then returns her attention back to Jayceon.

"In the meantime, your son has been selling dope and in the streets. I'm working two jobs, there's only so much that I can do here, Jay. Oh, and he's fucking." Deja now grew frustrated. She didn't understand why Jayceon came off so calm and meek about the situation.

Sighing, Jayceon turns to face Marterrio, a spitting image of himself only taking after Deja's smooth brown, skin complexion.

"Listen, son. There's nothing for you out here in these streets but either jail time or an early grave. You can't be out here in these streets; that's not the way to go. Your sisters need you. Your mom need you. And you need you to set an example for Raina and -"

"Raine," Deja corrects him.

"...Raine and Rylee," Jayceon continues. "And if I hear about you selling dope again, I'm going to kick your ass. And you out here messing around with these females. They don't come built like your mom anymore. You better be wrapping up out here and using a condom, you hear me boy?"

Deja could tell from Marterrio's posture that he didn't take the words of his dad seriously. She waits until Marterrio exits the kitchen and then says, "I had to hide the money and drugs from the cops for his ass! You could've at least sounded more serious."

"Deja, had you not moved away, you probably wouldn't have this problem out of him," he says.

"Are you kidding me right now? He was this way before we left! There were times when Marterrio would stay gone around the clock on me," she fussed and then deeply exhales.

"When he cuts up, you need to reach out to me. That's what we're doing, co-parenting. If you feel like you can't get through to him, call me, hell."

"I don't even think you're getting through to him," Deja thinks aloud. Maybe her son is almost too far gone in these streets. She now fears that they'll swallow him alive worse than her.

Leaving her first job, there was Cavius calling Deja. She didn't answer him until she was close to her car. "Hello?" Deja finally answers on the last ring.

"Hey, baby," he says on the other end with a smile on his voice.

"What I tell you about calling me that?" she grins to herself with a serious tone.

"What are you doing?" he goes on to ask her.

"Leaving work," Deja then turns the key in the ignition. Something different was going on with her car to not make it crank up. She knew she had put gas in it just yesterday, so that couldn't be the issue.

"How was work?"

"Hey, hold on," Deja calmly says and tried to crank her

car to life again. "Sure," Cavius hisses.

Please don't let this be happening to me! At a hundred and eight nine thousand miles, Deja has been holding onto her 2006 Toyota Camry for years now. She wasn't ready for a car note in her life.

Still on the phone with Cavius, frustrated with her forehead leaning against the steering wheel, Deja tries to crank her car one last time. It didn't make any kind of noise to at least attempt to turn over and come to life.

"Cavius?" Deja says with the phone to her ear again.

"I'm still here," he replies.

"I was trying to crank my car and it won't come on. I need a ride to my house," she sighs.

"Okay, where you at?"

"TR and Friends Cleaning Services over here off Poplar and White Station," she answers him.

"I'm on my way," he says.

This is a moment Deja is used to. After Jayceon and before she met Reese, Deja lost the engine to her last car on the interstate. A man was kind enough to pull over and offer his help, and that's how she met Reese.

Waiting for Cavius to arrive, Mr. Benson, her manager emerges from the building and walks up to Deja. He's about the same height as Deja, only wider and older. She didn't really like him cause she don't kiss ass. Mr. Benson had an infatuation for majority of the women he manages. Some have wanted Mr. Benson back for a trick and others have either complained on him or left their job.

That's how power works sometimes in the work field when you're relatives to the owners of the business. He almost tried to pull one on Deja and had the wrong bitch.

Sitting in her dead car with the door open, she looks up to him.

"Is everything alright here with your car?" he uses his

fore finger to push his glasses up on the bridge of his nose. She grew irritated just by his tendencies.

"It's dead, but I'm waiting on my ride," she replies.

"Oh, it's dead? Might be the battery. You need a boost off?"

"No I don't," she was blunt and irritated, keeping her sentences short with him.

"Do you have anyone on the way? You can't be on the lot like this or leave your car here," he says. Deja stands up from sitting down and then folds her arms across her breasts.

"Mr. Benson, my man is coming. He got this," she then waves her hand at him, returning to sit down again. The words "my man" had proudly rolled off the tip of Deja's tongue, but she thought otherwise.

Five minutes later, Cavius had pulled up in his BMW car that now looked like he had modified it a little. The headlights and wheels were different from the last time Deja seen the car. Huge and looking good like a bag of money, Cavius gets out from the driver seat and strolls over to Deja.

He wasn't fully her man just yet, but he might be. Cavius takes his big arms around Deja and hugs her. She closes her eyes, inhaling the warm and musk aroma of his expensive cologne, her hands landing along the ripples of his muscles.

"Okay, okay," Deja pulls away, gently patting her hands on his arms.

Cavius smiles from ear to ear and says, "I thought about you way before I called? I hope you like Christian Dior."

"I guess," Deja says. "I have to call for a tow truck right fast."

Cavius places his big hand over the screen of Deja

phone and says, "It's already been handled. Who's he?" The two of them both look towards the building where Mr. Benson was standing near the entrance doors.

"He's just my manager making sure I don't leave my car on the lot," Deja says and then turns away. Cavius walks with Deja over to the passenger side of the car and opens the door for her.

Lowering herself down into the car, the first thing Deja sees is a small, Macy's bag; it's sweet scent filling her nostrils. "Hm?" Deja moans, her undivided attention on the bag. She searches through the white, tissue paper until reaching a perfume set. Inside was a perfume, lotion and body wash box set of the latest release of Christian Dior with a set of 14k, small gold hoop earrings.

Did he really just bust an easy three hundred dollars on me just this fast, plus the fee for the tow truck?

Deja waits until Cavius gets into the car, joining her in the driver's seat. "You like your gift?" he asks.

"I-I-I can't take this, Cavius," Deja softly says.

"You know it's not nice to turn down a gift?" he gently smiles.

"Well my mom didn't teach me that," Deja says with bitterness and then sighs. Cavius did have a valuable point that makes sense to her. "I'm sorry. I've just kind of had a long day at work," she later adds.

"It's fine. It be like that sometimes," he continues to smile and then picks up his phone.

"But I'm trying to be your man, here." Deja acts like she ignores him and checks out her small gifts. Minutes later, the tow truck shows up, relieving Deja for the rest of the evening.

"You okay?" Cavius ponders, his voice low and calm. The leather interior of his car was shiny and new looking, with that new car smell mixed with sweet cologne that filled Deja's nostrils. She's even more better now that he came to her rescue and paid for a tow truck to get her car.

"I mean, I'm good. I'm just sitting here so puzzled about you. You're unusual," Deja glares his way.

"We should get to know each other more, you know," Cavius insists. Deja rolls her eyes, but smiles to herself.

"We can wait. I'm more concerned about how I'll get to my second job," she sighs, watching the cars past by her.

"You can borrow my car. I do have three more including the Corvette," Cavius suggests. Deja turns in her seat to face him.

"What are you hitting at? Like why are you so nice to me; is it because I'm a single mom with three kids? You've bought me this gift and paid for the tow truck. What's next? Why are you so...so..." Deja hesitated, she couldn't find the right word she was looking for.

"Why I'm so real to you? Cause you deserve a real man, Deja," Cavius calmly says. "You don't need anyone that's gonna come into your life with little boy games. You come with a package deal, and I'm all for it."

"But you don't know a thing about me or my past," she says.

"We all have a past."

"That's not it. Not if we're carrying our ways from the past," Deja concurs. Cavius gently sighs and remains silent.

Arriving at her place, Cavius turns to face Deja and says, "I can swing by and pick up and drop you off at your jobs if you want?"

"Only for tonight," Deja says. Marterrio's court date tomorrow was on the back of her mind, lingering in her thoughts. "My son has court tomorrow morning and..." once again, she couldn't find the rest of the words to say. Deja looks away from Cavius.

"I'm here for you, Deja. I'm here for the whole package," Cavius reaches over to hold her soft hand in his. As much as she wanted to remove her hand from his, she didn't.

"It's tomorrow at nine in the morning," Deja says. She really needs for Marterrio's father to go and just the two of them alone. The one more call-in rule still applied to her. One more call-in and she's out. "And I could end up being fired from my job."

"If anything tries to give you an ultimatum over itself or your kids, then you don't need it, Deja," Cavius says. He's right, but all the persuasion in the world couldn't convince Deja otherwise.

When they arrived at Deja's duplex, for her next question, she swallowed her pride. "Do you have anything planned between now or when school gets out?" Deja inquired.

"I really have a business luncheon planned at 2:30, so I was really hoping that you could get the car for a while," Cavius sternly looks over to Deja and says. She wished like hell he was just playing with her. What will her kids think if they see her pull up to get them in a brand new BMW.

"*I can't!*" Deja wants to yell at him in frustration. *Deja, shit is really still kind of hard for you right now… take this nigga help for* once, Deja's mind convinced her.

"I mean… really? We've moved onto a level where you're trusting me with your car," she gently smiles.

"My meeting will be an hour long. Maybe us and the kids can grab dinner at Olive Garden or somewhere," he says.

Olive Garden? Who in the hell eats at Olive Garden during a week day? Dinner at restaurants were reserved for good paydays and on a Friday with Deja.

"No, that's a fast approach. I'll start introducing you to

them slowly," she confirms. Cavius nods his head and then exits the car.

Deja gathered her purse and gift; she was just about to help herself out of the car until Cavius opens the door for her.

Climbing out of the car, Deja notices her neighbor's teenage daughter and friends watching them from across the yard. She wished like hell she would've seen how a man is supposed to treat a woman while coming up. Her mom could never keep a steady relationship.

"You wanna come in?" Deja turns to face him.

Cavius lifts his wrist with his fancy watch, glancing at the time and then says, "Sure, I have time."

Instead of jumping each other's bones, they sat in the living room with a cup of red wine and popcorn, one of Cavius's ideas towards relaxing after a long day at work. He really knew how to charm a woman.

Sitting across from each other with her legs rested on his, Cavius gently massages Deja's thigh. "So tell me more about you? Like your past," Cavius ponders.

"After you," she smiles. "You say your life wasn't always wealthy."

"It wasn't. I used to be the middleman of the dope game. Becoming the plug almost landed me ten years behind bars," he openly admits, holding Deja's gaze in his eyes. Her brows press together.

"Looks like everyone sold dope in their lifetime, huh?" she sits back.

"Have you?" Cavius asks her.

To tell the truth or not? "No, I just liked putting my hands on things that I wanted. My mom couldn't afford a lot of shit for me, so when I got older, I started stealing."

"And your kids? How old are they? What's their names?"

"I have a son and his name is Marterrio. And my two girls are by the same man – not Marterrio's dad – and their names are Raine and Rylee. My boy is seventeen-and-a-half, Raine is sixteen, and Rylee is five," she explains to him, loving her thigh massage.

"So you've just had a baby five years ago, huh? You want another one?" he jokes with her and then laughs at how Deja's face went cold. "I'm just kidding with ya!"

"Hehehe," she sarcastically laughs. "So how's the baby?"

"The baby's not here yet," Cavius calmly replies without looking at Deja.

"Why do you want to be serious with me and not with her? She's having your child," Deja asks him.

"She came into my life at a point when I needed comfort. I was fresh out of a relationship, vulnerable and in need of the attention she gave me. But she had a nasty habit when it came down to drugs. I call myself breaking up with her and about a month later, she texted me saying that she's pregnant," he explains to her.

"So, she's allegedly pregnant by you? You got money. Why not get one of those paternity tests?"

"There were…" Cavius clears his throats, "… Moments where we was intimate with each other before breaking up, so I'm halfway sure the baby is mine and then I'm not sure."

"The proof will be in the pudding then, won't it?" Deja raises an eyebrow. Cavius briefly turns his head away before returning his gaze to Deja.

"Right now, I want you to let me into your world. I want to be your man, Deja," he says again. Deja plays off her blush, moving her legs away from him.

"Look at the time? You better get going," she raises up

from the couch. Cavius quickly reaches out and grabs Deja's hand.

"Starting tomorrow morning, I'll clear my schedule to be with you and your son -"

"Whoa, pump your brakes okay. You are going sixty-five in a thirty-five speed limit zone. Let's take things slow when it comes down to my kids alright?" Deja firmly says. Cavius nods his head in response.

When Cavius gave the car over to Deja, she couldn't believe that she was behind the steering wheel of a BMW, and he made sure that the tank was full.

After picking up the kids from school, Deja utilized her time with the car by going shopping; she could use the retail therapy. There was nothing else that could take her mind off her son's court date like the way shopping could.

She didn't know how things would go on tomorrow morning, but she hoped like hell that he didn't mess his background up.

Four in the evening had rolled around and, without hearing any word from Cavius, Deja had went home to cook and prepare dinner with the help of Raine.

"So mom, where did you get the BMW from, huh?" Raine curiously asks Deja, now assisting with stirring the cornmeal batter. From her last experience, Raine first cracks an egg and then drops its yolk down into the batter.

"You wouldn't believe me if I told you that I have this friend and he cares for my well-being," Deja smiles to herself. Noticing Raine's eyes on her, Deja straightens up and then continues to strip the collard greens.

"A friend? I hope he's better than Big Doug," Raine says, stirring the bowl of cornbread batter.

"Oh, he's ten times better than Big Doug. He has another car that's a Corvette."

"So where you meet him? All I see you do is work and work," Raine asks.

"I met him at work. I wasn't going to give him a chance, but I'm glad that I did."

"Do you like him? Are you interested in him being a boyfriend? Will we like him?" Raine and Deja now were turned to face each other. Raine could see the glow in her mom's face at the thought of this mystery friend.

"Yes to the first question, and I'm not sure he'll accept me for my past as far as him being a boyfriend. So, you don't have to worry about question number three," Deja forces a smile.

"Mom, you need someone to make you happy… someone that'll take care of you for once," Raine then pulls her mom into her, and they exchange a brief hug before returning to cooking.

She made sure to have a nice and hefty dinner for her kids and also invited Jayceon over. Deja and Raine had cooked baked macaroni, collard greens with pig skin, black eyed peas, and cornbread with peppered steaks. Deja didn't know the outcome of tomorrow's court date, but she hoped like hell her son gets off free.

Chapter 6

"The state of Tennessee versus Marterrio Howard, by order of the court you are found guilty -"

Deja didn't flip or fold right away while she sat in the pupil section of the courtroom. Raine cuffed her mouth and her eyes filled with tears as Jayceon draped his arm around her.

"He's going to be okay," Deja could hear Jayceon say to Raine.

"... since this is your first offense, you'll serve a six-month term in the Shelby County jail and six months on parole after your release," the judge says with a stern face, his eyes fixed on Marterrio. The heat came from nowhere and got to Deja's head. She grew hot and nauseated, the buttons of her suit were too tight and her feet ache.

It's just six months! Deja tries to convince herself but fails. "I can't breathe," Deja whispers and gets up from her seat before the judge can adjourn the court. Seeing that Deja had no color in her face, the bailiff let her through. Jayceon and Raine followed after her.

Deja quickly undid her blazer and removed it, finding a nearby bench and sitting down. She uses her hands to fan herself as Jay and Raine arrives.

"Mom, what's wrong?" Raine ponders.

"Hot flash?" Jayceon asks her.

Holding up her hand, Deja says, "I dress him nice in a suit and tie with dress shoes for him to be sentenced to six months."

"You real petty for saying that," Jayceon says, backing away from her.

"I'm not petty for saying shit!" Deja yells at him. "I try to raise him to the best of my knowledge while you go and make a life, and this is what I get out of him. He's always in the streets."

"What you got your blood pressure up high for, Deja? I'll put the money on his books. It's only for six months," Jayceon says.

Without thinking, Deja raises her hand and slaps Jayceon. Six months? Christmas was right around the corner. Deja hated that her son had to learn the hard way. "You'll never understand," her voice breaking, Deja gets Raine by the hand and storms off.

For days, she had her phone on 'Do Not Disturb' when she was at the house and ignored incoming calls when she was at work. Now at the house with a full off day, the girls were at school and only one thing was on Deja mind to get her thoughts off Marterrio.

She rolls herself a blunt and pores a cup of brown liquor, filling the glass with ice. Just as Deja eases down to have a seat on the couch, someone gently taps on the security door. Pausing, she waits to see if they were going to knock again.

Tap! Tap! Tap!

87

"Shit," Deja sighs, and then gets up and goes over to the window. The first thing she spots is a new Mercedes-Benz in the yard, parked behind the BMW she still had the keys to in which Cavius couldn't get in touch with her to get back.

Tap, tap, tap, tap!

A few knocks goes again from the other side of the door.

"Who is it?" she yells.

"Cavius," he says. Deja sighs and then unlocks the door. Standing tall in casual clothing, Cavius had with him a bottle of wine and a bag of carry out from Olive Garden.

"What is this?" Deja asks him.

"I haven't heard from you in days, Deja. You won't answer your phone and you're barely at home. I miss you," he says. "What's going on with you?"

Inviting him inside, they have a seat over on the couch. Raw and herself, Deja continues to light her blunt, wanting for Cavius to have a problem with it. Sitting on the other side of the couch, Cavius had his plate and then hands Deja's hers.

"I hope you like Chicken Alfredo," he smiles at her. Deja sets her take out tray onto the edge of the end table, and then takes a pull from her blunt, still waiting on his reaction. "So tell me what's on your mind? You seem so tense," he scoots closer to Deja.

"I don't feel like talking about it," Deja gently groans.

"Does it have anything to do with your son? You never told me how his court date went."

Ignoring Cavius's concern, Deja takes another pull from the blunt. The two of them didn't touch their food until Deja felt comfortable around him again. As their food grew cold, Deja was finally ready to open up to him.

Massaging her feet, Cavius intensely watches Deja, studying her moods and what'll make her tick. "So, care to tell me now?"

"I guess so," Deja sighs. "Where do I start? Uh... my son is in jail as we speak and his dad is putting money on his books," she pauses, cuffing her mouth, tears filling her eyes. "I didn't even stay to see them take him out the courtroom! I didn't even visit him yet. I'm so disappointed," Deja briefly sobs and then pulls herself together.

Sniffling and wiping her eyes, she says, "I tell Marterrio about being in the streets all the time and where it'll get him. It's like he doesn't hear my voice getting through to him."

"Deja," Cavius softly calls. As he stops massaging, Cavius takes Deja's hands and holds them in his. His big hands were warm and soft. "Some experiences are better if it's through self-experience," he says.

"And what if he gets out and gets locked up again for something worse?" she asks Cavius.

"He won't," he says reassuringly with a soft smile on his face.

The two of them were about to hug when they both heard a loud crash noise from outside. Deja quickly turns her head to look towards the window as Cavius gets up from the couch. "Crazy neighbors?" he asks her, drawing the curtains back.

"I've never had a problem out of my neighbors or their business," Deja says.

"I know you're in there, Motherfucker!" a woman's voice shouts. Cavius' brows press together and he rushes over to the front door.

"Stay here!" he orders Deja. She watches him flee out the house.

Oh hell no! Deja frowns, standing behind the security

door, seeing a scenario of Cavius and some woman outside unfold in front of her.

"What the hell are you doing here?!" Cavius yells at the woman. She could've been at least five foot four inches solid tall, with a large belly and long weave that flowed down her back. Had to be this nigga baby momma?

"I don't know! You tell me? What the fuck you doing here at this bitch house?" she points her short finger at Deja's duplex. "You avoid me for what?"

"Taleah, you need to go," Cavius firmly says to her. Taleah dodges Cavius who tries to grab her. Picking up a brick, she runs and tosses it towards the front door. It lands on the porch step. "Taleah!" Cavius yells.

Spotting Deja, she taunts her, "Yea! You broke bitch! I see you!"

Her heart was racing, her hands clutched together in tight fists; Deja now had a disgusted look on her face. She had a feeling inside her that she couldn't shake off.

Deja opens the front door and sprints for Taleah, catching up and grabbing a handful of her hair. "Ladies! Deja, wait!" Cavius calls from the other side of the lawn.

"What's that's you say bitch?!" Deja then takes her hand and connects it to Taleah's mouth, busting her lip.

"Let me go! Help!" Taleah screams.

"Let her go, baby! You can't do this right here! Not with her," Cavius tears them apart. High and a little tipsy, Deja gives in and walks away. She can't fight Taleah the way she wants to anyway.

"I'm calling the police! She slapped me!" Taleah cries. "Look at my lip!" she touches her face.

"You don't come around my shit busting out nobody windows!" Deja turns around to argue at Taleah.

"I hope you have some bail money, bitch!" Taleah threatens Deja, who walks towards her front door.

"Oh, you still talking shit?" Deja marches over towards them, changing tracks.

Cavius takes Taleah by the arms and force her into her car, "Go mane!" He turns around to stop Deja in enough time, "Stop! Stop! Stop."

"Fool, don't tell me to stop! My son is locked up! I need a car! My money is running low! I got problems! I'll kick her pregnant ass!" Deja looks him in the eyes and says.

"No you won't!" Cavius says, his voice direct.

"She don't want these problems, Cavius," she growls at Cavius, and then snatches away from him. "Is she leaving or what?" Deja yells, walking away with Cavius trailing after her.

"No, it looks like she's calling the police," he says.

"Well, let them come!" Deja waves her hand in midair, continuing to walk away.

Like the scary bitch she is, Taleah waits in the car for the police to arrive, talking to them first while Cavius waits outside talking to another cop about Taleah busting the passenger side windows of his car. Reaching Deja, they find the brick that was used.

Talking to a cop while watching Taleah at the same time, Deja hears her tell them she and Cavius had attacked her.

"That's not what happened!" Cavius raises his voice. "I'm here with Deja, my new girlfriend… somehow she finds out and busts my car windows," he now calms down.

"No, that's not true!"

"Ma'am, are you lying to us? Cause we've seen a lot of scenarios of this situation before," one of the officers says to Taleah, his hands fixed on his hips.

"I tell you what. We're taking both of y'all to jail," a Black officer says with a firm tone, pointing one finger at Taleah and the other one at Deja.

"What?" Taleah frowns, now speechless. Deja's eyes were fixed on Taleah as they were both being handcuffed and being read their Miranda rights.

Deja's mind drifted back to when she first went to jail for shop lifting, after she had Marterrio. Her first night was rough and she clashed heads in jail with a veteran inmate. With a small frame, Deja had to fight the woman on behalf of respect, gaining it once she won. She ended up being in isolation for almost a whole month with no phone calls, no commissary from Jayceon, and no freedom. Not saying that jail made her tough, but it help her always prepare for the next time she ended up there.

Most women land themselves in jail and they can't handle it. They freak out and cry or go off to themselves and cry. Being confined inside a bedroom is better than being behind a locked cell door. The prison wards tell you what to do, when to leave your pod or go back to it. Some inmates kiss their asses. And when one gets into a physical altercation, the correction officers tries to restrains you but when they can't, they take out the mace.

Deja just knew that she wasn't getting out anytime soon. She sat on one side of the holding cell while Taleah was on the other. There was a White, young woman that was about to go crazy... hysterically crying and hitting the bars as she paces the floor back and forth.

Five hours into sitting down, a bailiff walks over to the holding cell and says, "Deja Crenshaw?! Come with me." Ready to get this day over with, Deja follows behind the bailiff, leading the opposite way from the screening room. Silent and without word, Deja follows the bailiff back out the way she came from, walking her through the exit doors and out into the lot.

The sun was settling into the sky. Red, orange, and blue

colors soaring across the evening sky. On the other side of the lot stood a figure leaning against his car she'd always recognize from afar.

"Cavius? You bailed me out?" she asks him, her brows pressed together. "I slapped your child's mother?"

"Some bitches deserve to be slapped by another woman," he shrugs his shoulders.

Deeply exhaling the evening fresh air, Deja smiles to herself and says, "Thank goodness it's not a school day. I have to report to court in the morning." She shakes her head from side to side, emotional at the thought of losing her job. They let her slide by with Marterrio's court date.

"It's okay, Deja. Let's just get inside the car and talk about it." Deja nods her head in agreement.

They didn't speak to each other until Cavius' car reached three miles away from Jail East. Deja begins, taking a deep breath and then asks, "How in the hell did she know where I live at?"

"She must've followed me," Cavius bluntly replies. "I don't know Deja, but I do apologize."

"No, don't. Because if she ever come to me wrong again and disrespects me and she's not pregnant, I'm going to dog walk that bitch right by her tracks. Y'all don't know me!"

"Damnit, Deja. I've been trying to get to know you. Every time I think you've opened up to me, you don't! I don't have a problem with accepting women the way they are, Deja," Cavius fumes. Deja deeply sighs.

"You're a wealthy and established, Black man, Cavius. If you knew the things about me that I knew, you wouldn't want to be with me anymore," Deja sighs.

"You really think so?"

"Yea!"

93

"Surprise me then, Deja. I've fucked with sluts, pocket pickers, and women that done drugged a guy before to steal his wallet! Even high dollar call girls; heartless ass women! What's so terrifying that you got on them, huh?"

"And look at you now? You're not with any of them!"

"You're right, but me and those women didn't break up on bad terms! I'm not with them anymore because they chose to walk away. Are you going to do the same to me?"

"What?" Deja asks. Taken by surprise, she embraces herself and presses her hands against the dashboard. The tires of Cavius's car loudly screeched against the road before coming to a complete stop. "What the hell?"

"I'm really feeling you, Deja, and I'd wish you just let me inside," he sighs and continues driving.

"So, did you get your windows fixed?"

"There was nothing to it," Cavius answers.

"What you doing tonight?" he later asks her.

"Nothing, probably drinking and going to sleep," her attention was looking out the window, her mind drifting onto her son.

"We need to check out this club in the wall called The Spot," he says. "Have you heard of it before?"

"Nope."

"Are you game?" That's when they both exchanged glances with each other and Cavius widely grins before turning his eyes back on the road. She's heard that phrase before from another nigga of the same physique nature.

"You giving me two ounces for one-fifty?" Deja's brows pressed together in confusion. He wasn't a normal plug to her, considering he'd give her two ounces for the low.

"Because you mom deuce, baby," he smiles big, stretching his arms out wide. "I fuck with you. So, are you game?"

"What kind of question is that? Hell yeah I'm down," she says, happily accepting the large, hand size bag of marijuana from Cane.

94

Deja nearly slumps down into her seat. *Please don't tell me this Cane nigga is related to Cavius?*

"You good? You acting like I said some wrong?" he asks her.

"Um, sure. I'll go. What time is you talking about going?"

"Eleven Tonight," he replies.

Okay, whatever!

For the rest of the evening, Deja had sage burning while she waltzed around with her face mask on and wearing a robe. She dedicated her time alone to herself this evening, even falling asleep in the tub before getting ready to go clubbing with Cavius. This should be something she's used to.

Big Doug loved going to the club; whether it was a strip joint or a party club, Deja would be right beside him enjoying the night life. Reese, on the other hand, loved those bar and grill type of environments, and he loved going to Hooters to watch the game and eat hot wings. But Jayceon, he enjoyed going to all kinds of parties in general. All these men in her timeline are different in some sort of way.

Deja couldn't believe that she was seeing the day that Cavius is dressed up in a graphic shirt and cut pattern pants with Jordan's on. But he didn't make Deja feel overdressed in any way, as she was wearing her sheer, black dress with a bra and thongs covering her lady parts. Deja remained standing still as Cavius walks up to her, his cologne getting the best of her juices. Cavius takes his hands behind Deja and pulls the curly locks of her hair around to drape past her shoulders.

"You look amazing and sexy," he smiles.

Deja grins, checking out how in heels, she's still not

taller than him. She loves that in a man. "I'm still not taller than you."

"It's okay love," he says. "Let's get going."

When they arrived at the club, Cavius took Deja by the hand. They went inside and walked straight to the VIP section. He held her hand until she sat down into her seat. A young woman with all black on approaches them right away with a menu and lingers behind, her wandering eyes checking out Cavius as his eyes were fixed on the menu before them.

"You want anything?" he leans over and asks Deja, resting his big, warm hand on her thigh.

"Uh yea, I'll take a shot of Jack and some mozzarella cheese sticks. I hope they're good," she says.

"Three shots of Jack Daniels with mozzarella sticks and twenty piece hot wings," he says to the girl. She scribbles down their order and then outstretches her hand for the menu from him. "Aht! Aht, we might order some different off this later," he says to the girl with a fatherly tone, making Deja snicker. The waitress swings around hard with an attitude, her braids flailing in midair.

"She did not appreciate that shit," Deja laughs as the girl switches away, her hips swaying from side to side.

"She'll be alright," Cavius waves his hand and relaxes back into the booth seat.

She wondered why he ordered three shots of Jack, taking two of them by himself straight to the head. Deja didn't know what to think of it.

Once they've eaten and had liquor in their system, Cavius and Deja went down to the dance floor. Cavius has the moves that matched Deja's, with the look and swag. Together they had a good time. He took her mind off a lot of things, her son being in jail for one.

The following morning, Deja slips into a casual dress

shirt and slacks with flat, ballerina shoes for her court date. Cavius was in the living room making a phone call. With her hair clamped up, Deja glances at her reflection in the mirror one last time. From the corner of her eye, she spots Cavius and says, "I thought you were still on the phone."

"Listen, Deja," he says walking over to her. "I'm close friends with the judge that you're going to see in another hour, and I worked in a favor for you. No more slapping pregnant women, okay?" Cavius holds up his finger at Deja.

She giggles and lowers his hand, "Okay, but after she drops and gets wrong with me again, I won't be so nice like I was the first time."

"Deal then, but in the meantime, cool it," he then leans in and kisses her on the lips. "Let's get you going."

"You're not coming?" she inquires, following after him.

"Nope, you're good. I have a meeting in another forty-five minutes," Cavius briefly glances back at her and says.

"And the car?"

"You can keep it, Deja," he smiles.

Deja had to first face the judge, who didn't charge her with anything except warned her that if she does it again, he'll put her away for five years. When she walked out onto the lot, Deja had encountered Taleah.

Taleah leans against the fender of the car with her arms folded atop her big belly and a smug grin on her face. *Damn she looks like she could be due in any minute.*

"Can you go on about your way?" Deja asks her as nice as she can… before she gone and run her ass over!

Taleah suckles her teeth and says, "So, Cavius helped you, huh?"

"Maybe the judge just knows that you're one of those worrisome ass baby mommas," Deja says with acid in her tone.

"You don't have any idea of the man you're dealing with. Stay away from him, whatever your name is!"

"And if I don't, what you're supposed to do? Fight me?" Deja meddles her and then unlocks the car door. Taleah stands out of the way, gently nodding her head and sucking her teeth again. Deja pulls off from the parking spot, clutching the steering wheel. *Bitch!*

Sitting across from the small screen, Deja glances around and sees how other women were already talking to the men they had come to visit. Minutes later, the screen comes on, showing Marterrio in a light blue, short sleeve scrub shirt and a white, long sleeve shirt underneath it. His hair was cut low in a fade, and as black as her son is, Marterrio had a bruise under his left eye.

Smiling from ear to ear, he says, "Hey, ma."

"Hey baby," she smiles in return, tears forming in her eyes. Deja ain't seen her little man in almost three months. After making things officially serious with her relationship with Cavius, Deja finally brought herself to seeing Marterrio.

Ignoring his eye, she says, "How you been? Have your dad been taking care of you in here?"

"Yea, and there's something else," he says and sighs. Marterrio's eyes fell down low before returning back to the screen.

Please don't let him say that someone done made him they bitch!
Please don't let him say that someone done made him they bitch!

"What is it, Marterrio?" Deja asks him.

"You remember Denise from Georgia?"

Deja squints her eyes at him, shifting uncomfortably in her chair, "No, her name doesn't ring a bell. What about this Denise?"

"I was gone move in with her before we got put out," he says.

Deja shifts different in her chair again, her memory recalling the name Denise. Her name was distant.

"Mom, she's pregnant by me. I have a baby on the way with her," he says through the phone receiver. Something in the air had grasped Deja by the throat; she couldn't speak anymore. Her thoughts scattered around her head. She couldn't fathom the thought of her son having a baby with a female she hardly knew of!

"What?" Deja's brows press together. "Hold up, wait. What you say now?"

"Mom, I need you to understand something. I wasn't always out there selling dope. I was with Denise for some of those nights, and now we have a kid on the way," he says again.

"Let me get this right? So, you just been out here fucking with no rubber like you're grown -"

"Ma, I need you to save all that for later. Denise isn't out here like how you was with my dad. She's about to graduate with her associates in Nursing," he proudly says. Deja swallows hard and deeply exhales. If she could've breathed smoke from her nostrils, there would be some.

Swallowing her anger, she says, "Well congratulations son." *But you still don't know these bitches out here!* "When you're out, if it's possible, I would love to actually meet her. Does your dad know?"

As Marterrio hesitates answering his mom, Deja sighs and breaks eye contact from him. A voice in the receiver says, "You now have five minutes left."

"Well, I wish you were here for your birthday and Christmas coming up, Marterrio."

"I am here, mom. They didn't put me in another city. I'm not dead in my grave. I'm still here. I wish you could bring my sisters to see me."

"I can't bring them to see you like this," she says. *"Good bye!"* the female voice intrudes again as Marterrio parts his lips to say something to his mom. He hates these things and he hates that he's in jail. The food is awful; the only thing that edible is the commissary his dad or Denise orders to send him and making noodles with hot chips. Jail is worse than surviving in the streets. He had to learn and maneuver new ways of surviving inside and avoiding fights with gang members is one that he hasn't mastered yet.

As soon as Deja got back to the car, the first number she dials is Jayceon. After the second ring, he answers the phone with a lot of different noises in the background.

"Yea, what's up baby momma?"

"You knew?!" she yells into the phone speaker. Deja's blood pressure was instantly up.

"Knew about what?" he chuckles. "Yea man, set it over there! Aye you, be careful with that, and don't break my thousand dollar speakers. That's your paycheck!" he orders around a few people.

"That Marterrio got some female out here pregnant and I've never met the woman a day in my life!" she fussed at him.

"Deja, you're gonna have to learn how to relax."

"I've been relaxing, Jayceon!" she yells. "Being easy on him got him in the shit he's in now! He won't be 18 until three more weeks from now and he think he's a man!"

"He's a young man. I didn't say anything because of how good he talked about the woman. I think she and the baby can be a turning point for him."

"You don't really know your son! And that's if the baby is his!"

"Oh my god! Talking to you is useless sometimes. Are you done?"

"Some dad you are! Either you're going to guide him right from wrong or leave him the hell alone. Being proud of being allegedly a father isn't good for him. Did you forget? Having Marterrio wasn't a turning point for *us*!" she then hangs the phone up in his face with her final thoughts. Jayceon being the guy that he is, calls back. Deja doesn't answer and puts her phone on 'Do Not Disturb' mode right away.

With it being so early in the day, instead of going straight to her duplex, Deja flocks over to Cavius's office also grabbing him lunch from McAllister's. The secretary, Heather, had a distinct look on her face as they now stood across from each other.

"You know who I'm here to see. You've seen my face before, Heather," Deja firmly says.

"I know that. It's just that Mr. St. Claire is busy at the moment. He's been held up in his office in a private meeting for an hour now. He's not expecting you, Miss Deja."

"He's not expecting me?" Deja suckles her teeth. "What's with all the extra stuff then?"

"Miss Deja, it's best that you leave and come back later," she says, her bright green eyes fixed on Deja.

Since when? Deja hadn't come into his office often, but when she does, Cavius always makes time to see her.

"I see," she says, conducting her growing frustration. Deja calmly places the basket down as soft as she could with a fake smile. She then turns and walks away, strutting out of the office lobby area.

Her next stop was a place that she hadn't been to in two months. Parking her car at the edge of the sidewalk, Deja gets out and then strolls up the pavement. She gently knocks onto the sturdy wood with her knuckles and then waits.

Cane opens the door with his big body build and a smile, "Hey, mom deuce!" He then invites her inside.

"What do you have for me, Cane?" Deja asks him, leaning against the work table with stacks of cash along the middle of the surface.

"You know what I got for you, baby," he takes his hand and grabs onto his crotch, teasing her like he always would.

"Oh my goodness, not that!"

"Damn baby, you hurt my feelings when you say it like that. What you got up for tonight?"

"Working," she says.

"After that?"

"Sleeping, why? You didn't even answer my question first nigga!"

Cane chuckles and widely grins, "Okay, you right. I have a delivery of ten keys that's happening when you get off from work. You make the drop, and you get twenty percent out of it."

"Is that right?" Deja asks. Cane walks closer up to her, stepping under the same light as she was. They were so close, Deja could smell his warm cologne and clean breath. There was also something else about his eyes and nose that reminds her of someone else.

"I got what you need, baby," Cane's voice was now low, melting down her throat like honey. His hands roaming her thighs and then to her ass, harshly pulling her close to his hard chiseled chest.

"Mm?" Deja raises a brow. "And that is?"

"How does ten grand sounds, mom deuce?"

"The type of stacks I need in my life right now," she looks Cane in the eyes, and there she sees something again, a tiny sparkle of a flame.

"You make the drop and it's yours," he says into her ear and then holds Deja closer. She forcefully shoves him off her, later pointing her forefinger at Cane. With his silver and diamond crusted grill in his mouth, he grins; he likes that shit!

"You such a naughty little mom," Cane rubs his hands together.

"Hands off, boss," Deja teases him, fixing her body into a sexy pose as she pretends to fix her hair that didn't need to be fixed.

"I'll call you when it's time, mom deuce," Cane says, remaining where he stood. Deja grins and then walks away. Every now and then, she needed only validation from a hard nigga like Cane to remind her that she still got it.

For the rest of the day, Deja didn't hear from Cavius which wasn't like him. Since they've gotten serious, he's made less of an effort towards reaching out to Deja and having her in his company. He hadn't even popped up yet to massage her feet or cook for her and the girls as he normally would. She needed his presence on today after visiting her son.

On her second job, Deja was three hours into her shift that was almost over and her night couldn't get any more boring. She was used to seeing the usual customers with their families or couples that made the restaurant their favorite place to eat. She was used to seeing a male customer with a different female from the last time, and treating her better than the last one.

As she exited the kitchen area and walked into the dining room with her table's food, she wasn't expecting to see Cavius standing near the hostess booth with an entirely different woman beside him. She was stunning with a nicer rack of breasts than Deja; the shape of her body was amazing.

What the fuck?

Her blood boils and her spine cringes as her legs stiffens. Deja couldn't decide if she wanted to keep things professional for the sake of keeping her job or if she wanted to knock everything over!

"Keep calm, honey bee. I'm pretty sure it's just business," Melissa says into Deja's ear before rushing away, being their designated server for the night.

"*I'll keep calm alright!*" Deja thinks to herself and continues walking.

Moving around as she should, Deja breathes slowly with every step, trying her hardest not to stare so hard. So many questions and suspicions filled her head. She couldn't wait to return to the back to catch up with Melissa.

"Well, what do you think about it? Cause I'm about to explode and not give two fucks!" Deja says as they met up in the walk-in refrigerator.

"She's beautiful for one thing, but I don't know Deja. Your mountain is a charmer," she admits.

"Let me serve them!"

"You don't need to do anything stupid until you know for sure!"

"What I know is that he didn't let me bring him lunch earlier today and, on top of that, he's a no call and a no show! I've brought this man around my kids and shit. I think I need answers," Deja fumes and then deeply exhales.

"No honey! What you won't do is let this man come up in here with some plastic Barbie and disturb your money flow. Either do your job or clock out for the night if you feel as though it's gonna cost you losing this job!"

"I don't give a fuck about this job! As fast as I found this one, I can get another one."

Melissa folds her arms across her breasts and says, "Deja, I love you and you're my favorite co-worker, but you can't let this man mess it up for you. My nana once told me that a man gone always do him! You better do you." Melissa then places her hands on her hips.

"But at my place of work, Melissa?"

"Better here than where you lay your head."

Still hot and turning on her heels, Deja exits the walk-in refrigerator. Slowly going out into the hallway, she peers over to the other side of the room where they sat at a table off to themselves. He was making her laugh and blush at the same time. It wasn't until Cavius' eyes met her gaze that he lifts his hand and waves at her. *The nerve!*

Deja doesn't return a wave, spinning around on her heels. She removes her apron, grabs her coat and then clocks out with no intention of leaving in peace. Hot tears streaming down her face and with the tip of her car key, Deja walks around Cavius's new BMW truck, scratching its lovely, silver paint. She would've done more had a couple not exited the building. Deja gets in her car and then leaves.

Laid across the bed, Deja didn't want to think about Cavius and whatever he had going on with that other bitch. She was ready to get money. She changed her clothes, dressing in a baggy pullover with black jeans and then pulls her hair into a tight bun, later hearing her cell phone ringing.

"Hello?" Deja answers.

"You ready?" Cane's voice says.

"Just tell me where to go."

"Meet me at the old Meat Factory," he says and then hangs up.

Easing through the streets with the cops on the prowl in their squad cars, Deja made it to the old meat warehouse. She wasn't alone, seeing Cavius' car with another.

"This is Lil Jake," Cane introduces him. "He's going to be following from afar for back up. Things have just gotten dangerously heated, mom deuce. You sure you want to do this?"

"I've gotten out of my bed and I'm here now. There's no turning back."

"You're going to give a guy named Yo this bag, and he's going to give you one back. That's it. No conversation, just straight exchanging, alright?"

"Yea," she nods her head.

"A lot of people will turn for thirty thousand dollars; be careful. Lil Jake, make sure nothing happens to her, you hear me?"

The boy looked like he was no older than her own son. Deja rolls her eyes and then walks away, later driving off into the night.

She ain't never did no shit like this before. As she went further down the dark road with high beam lights on and the radio off, Deja was getting a gut feeling in her stomach. The only thing she needed was peace and concentration, knowing that she had a large bag of cocaine beside her in the passenger seat. Deja deeply inhales and then exhales, clutching the steering wheel.

Minutes later, a pair of headlights in the opposite direction were approaching her. Deja waits for the cue, seeing that it stops first. She then pulls up closer, just in case she needed to run.

Her heart's beating fast but her thoughts were intact as she reaches over and grabs the bag. The man gets out the other car first with his duffel bag, strolling over to Deja before she could leave the car.

Remaining in her seat with the doors locked, Deja rolls down the window. The exchange was quick, the two of them handing one bag to each other. Something didn't feel right about the bag from holding it by its handles. It's weight didn't match what Deja would expect.

She opens the bag and then checks it, seeing that it wasn't the amount of money she looked forward to. Deja quickly exits the car and says, "Aye! Where's the rest of the money?"

"No more money. That's all you get!" he says and then rushes away. Deja got out the car and then pursues after him as he runs back to his vehicle. Close on him, Deja harshly shoves the short, foreign guy to the ground. As he falls over, the bag flies from his hand and Deja mounts him.

"Where's the rest of it, huh?" she then takes her fist and punches him in the face.

"In-in-in the car!" he stammers, pointing his finger on the side of them at the car. "It's in the car! Front seat."

Deja punches him again, and then gets up, hearing Lil Jake pull up behind the vehicle she drove. "Deja? What's taking so long!" he calls from afar. Deja continues over to the car and then goes into the front seat. There was the rest of the money. She quickly snatches the money and then turns to face Lil Jake.

Frowning, he says, "What the fuck is you doing?"

"Watch how you talk to me!" Deja scolds him.

"Bitch, you ain't my momma!" he then reaches down at the money in her hands. "Gimme this shit!"

"And you ain't my son! But I'mma whoop your ass like yo mammy should've!" Deja stomps onto his toes and then takes her elbow across his face. Lil Jake stumbles back and then withdraws his gun from behind him. Deja pauses, catching her breath.

"You gone shoot me, huh?"

"Cause you fucked up in the head! This ain't yo place, mom deuce," he yells at Deja, and then takes the gun and slaps her with it; she fell against the car, nearly inside of it. Silent and thinking with her face burning from the whack,

Deja watches as Lil Jake storms away and then effortlessly shoots the other guy. As hard as she wanted to play like it didn't get the best of her, she couldn't believe that he did that! Deja cuffs her mouth, seeing a pool of blood fill around his head.

While she was still speechless, Lil Jake takes the money from Deja's hands and fusses, "We couldn't send him back alive! If Cane asks, tell him the truth and he'll understand. Tell him that he attacked you when you found out what he was up to."

"If I don't?" Deja challenges him. Lil Jake grabs a handful of her pullover and then pulls her close to him.

Pressing the mouth of the gun to her head, Lil Jake looks her in the eyes and says, "Because if you don't, I'll have Marterrio killed in jail with one call. Then I'll come for your fine ass daughter and put a bullet between her head after I fuck the shit out of her! I'll throw little Rylee in the Mississippi River and make you watch her drown to her fucking death! That's what gone happen."

"Alright!" Deja snatches away from Lil Jake and then shoves him.

"You're so fucking beautiful! Why do you do this crazy shit?" he asks as Deja turns on her heels and walks away. Ignoring him, Deja retrieves the money bag and tosses it to him. She then gets into the car and drives off.

They didn't meet up with Cane until an hour later from the exchange. Deja's face still was aching and throbbing with pain and now had swelling in the area where she was hit. Cane had his eyes fixed on her as Lil Jake gave him the bag of money and the bag of cocaine. That's when he took his eyes off her and looks over to Jake.

"What the fuck is this? You bringing me back two bags instead of one," Cane says. Deja walks over to them. "And what happened to your face? What the fuck happened?" Cane turns to face Deja and says.

"He tried to short you," she interjects, and then sighs. "When I caught onto him, he attacked me."

"Yo, I don't like it when I'm being lied to. How the fuck am I supposed to clean this mess. Who shot him, huh?"

"I did," Lil Jake admits. Neither of them didn't see it coming when Cane took his whole hand and slaps the spit right out of Jake's mouth. He stumbles over, quickly regaining his balance. Deja didn't feel not one ounce of sympathy for the kid; he had a foul attitude and mouth!

"Just stupid! Now I have to explain to the boss man why this drop went south!" Cane yells at them both.

"Listen! Listen!" Deja grabs Cane by the face and forces a smile. "He tried to short change you, Cane. We were just looking out for you, that's all," she convinces him. Deja needed the money more than anything; it was time to run again.

"You really know how to calm my ass down, huh?" Cane says, leaning in closer to Deja. "Look at that bruise, mom deuce. I don't appreciate that shit! I ask that lil fucker to keep you safe and some nigga messes up your face," he takes the palm of his thumb and gently soothes it over Deja's bruise.

"It's okay, come on," Deja tugs at Cane's hands. He couldn't turn away from Lil Jake. "Cane? Come on," Deja urges him again, tugging harder. Cane breaks eye contact with Lil Jake and follows behind Deja.

They leave together with the two duffle bags, leaving Lil Jake to clean up the vehicles. "Mom deuce, you don't get it! I should've never chose that lil snake ass nigga!" Cane says from the driver's seat, mashing his foot on the gas pedal. Cane was going at least ninety in a sixty-five miles per hour zone.

"Well, it's over with now," Deja says. That's when Cane smashes onto the breaks, nearly throwing Deja into the windshield.

"It's not over with. The Pit Boys gonna wanna know what the fuck happened to their middle guy? He been doing exchanges and moving dope for as long as I've been in the business. We had a partnership with them niggas," Cane says with a serious look on his face.

"I'm telling you, Cane. That mane wanted some cut from the money to himself!"

"I get that, but they won't. Look what he did to your face! How I know if he's really dead?" Cane reaches over and gently touches the swollen bruise on the side of Deja's face; she winces at his touch. Deja takes his hand in hers. Somehow, it had a mind of its own, grabbing a handful of Deja's breast.

"You would've shot him instead?" she asks him. *"You need to shoot Lil Jake,"* is what she really wanted to say.

"Damn real for putting his hands on you like that!" he honestly says. "The only place where a man should touch a woman is here," his hand briefly squeezes her breast, then moves down to her stomach and pelvis. "And here," Cane gently says, causing a tingling sensation in Deja's. Without warning, he leans into her, and Deja meets him halfway.

His hands freely roams and touches on Deja's body as they passionately kiss each other. It hurt her face like hell to move her jaws, but the pain felt so good at the same time.

At the alarming sound of his cell phone ringing from the middle console, resting inside the cup holder, Cane tears away from her. They held each other's gaze until Deja breaks her eye contact first, her eyes going down to the uncanny and familiar number on his phone screen.

"Yea?" Cane says after taking a deep breath. "Nah man, I was just getting too worked up that's all," he says to the caller, settling into the driver's seat. Deja was taking her forefinger and wiping away the residue of his wet kisses from around her lip.

"I'll be around in thirty minutes," he later says and changes the gear shift into drive. Deja deeply exhales as Cane hangs up the phone.

Chapter 7

Sitting across a televised screen from her son, Deja picks up the receiver. Marterrio sees the worried look on her face when she didn't smile.

"Two times in one week?" he says on the line.

Deja sighs, and asks him, "Who is Lil Jake to you?"

"Who?"

"Lil Jake," she repeats herself.

Marterrio's brows press together and he answers, "He's a part of Cane's crew. How do you know him?"

"It's a long story, but I just need you to keep an eye open for yourself in there. Those prison guards can't protect you."

"I been found that out," Marterrio scoffs. "How's my sisters?"

"They miss you," she says, her eyes drifting down to the worn and written over wooden edge. Lil Jake had a bad way of reminding Deja to keep her mouth close; it's becoming harassment to her.

"Mom? What's wrong?" Marterrio asks her.

"Nothing, I just wish you was free," her eyes returns to the screen.

"Three more months and I will be," he grins on the screen.

When she returned home, she didn't expect Cavius to be parked in her yard like he was welcomed over. Deja intentionally parked on the curb as Cavius gets out the truck, looking tall and strong; his muscular physique made her pussy throb. She had to ignore the feeling between her legs and think with her head this go round.

"Good afternoon," he smiles at Deja as she approaches him.

"What the hell you doing here, Cavius?" she asks him, jumping straight to the point. Cavius continues to smile and chuckle.

"I've been busy over these few days, and I seen the way you looked at me the night before last," Cavius answers her. "It's not what you were thinking."

"Motherfucker, you could've took the bitch to anywhere that night but where I work at!" Deja fusses at him.

Cavius steps up to Deja and faces her, then says, "You didn't have to key my car, Deja. I really don't owe you an explanation of my business but I'm not screwing anyone neither."

What the fuck?! She lifts her hand to slap him, but Cavius grabs the same hand by the wrist, stopping her. Her brows pressed together and she makes eye contact with him. Cavius now had a serious look on his face and then says, "I'm damn sure not about to stand here and let you slap me. Come on and take a ride with me."

"Hell no!" Deja says, attempting to jerk her hand free from his tight grip. Cavius tilts his head, observing her face closer than before.

"So what happened to your face, hm? Looks like you been busy too over these few days. You got somebody on the side that was mad or some?"

"What? Hell no!" she answers, still trying to jerk her hand free. "Let me go, Cavius!"

Looking past her yard and judging the actions of an unmarked vehicle on the opposite side of the street, Cavius orders her, "I said get in the fucking car!"

Seeing the car moving and the passenger side windows rolling down, Cavius quickly pry open the rear seat door and picks Deja up. He tosses Deja across the backseat and then lays on top of her, leaving the door wide open as loud gunshots fired off. Cavius tucks his legs, getting into a hunch like position over Deja and covering her ears with her hands.

Deja could've sworn she was screaming, but she couldn't hear herself. The rear window shattered and the car shook from side to side. Deja couldn't tell if she or Cavius had been hit by a bullet or not! The rain of gunshots ends three minutes later, followed by the loud screeching noise of car tires against the pavement.

"Shit!" Cavius says, now sitting atop of Deja, forgetting his heavy weight was pressed against her.

"I think I can't breathe!" she could see herself saying but her mouth couldn't let the words out. Deja was in total shock. Of all her days of bad deeds, she's never been this close to losing her life! What she did in Georgia don't count because she was on foot and got away. What if they were in her duplex when the drive by happened?

"Deja, baby? You alright?" he asks her, now climbing off her.

"I-I-I don't know," she stammers.

Cavius glares around, seeing her neighbors come outside. He had to think fast, not wanting to deal with the police… him or Deja couldn't. This was now a street war going on.

"I'm going to need you to get your head together, Deja! Look at me!" he says, placing his huge hands on the sides of her face. Cavius could see the shock all over her face still. He overlooks Deja and gets out the truck. Getting back into the driver's seat, Cavius cranked the vehicle. Reaching the street, he sped down the road.

Deja assumes he's just driving fast to get them away from the area, until he caught up with the vehicle that shot at them. "Cavius? What are you doing? Is you crazy?" Deja steadied herself in between the driver and passenger seat, her hand rapidly tapping Cavius on the shoulder.

"Just sit back," he says in a low, firm tone, using his elbow to move her back. Cavius then reaches over to the glove compartment, retrieving a gun with a long barrel.

"Cavius?" Deja calls, her tone a little softer than before, her mind racing and unsure of what's to come next.

With his hands clutching the steering wheel, Cavius rams the passenger side of the car into the shooters. When the driver in the car rolls down the window, Cavius fires in one aim at him.

Deja's eyes grew wide and she cuffs her mouth as the shooters car spiral out of control until someone else took over the steering wheel.

"This is crazy!" Deja shouts at him.

"Just sit the fuck back!" Cavius yells, and then starts firing again, killing the next guy.

She had a gut feeling that Cavius' gun had a whole mag in the bottom of it and he wasn't going to stop until it was emptied or until everyone in the other car was dead. Deja now turns around, facing the rear windshield, seeing how the car didn't completely stopped until it's front end

115

had hit the guard rail. Cavius kept speeding down the road.

At the alarming sound of nearby police sirens, he reduces his speed. What she just seen, Deja couldn't play it off and act normal. She slumped down into her seat where they couldn't see her.

This man is crazy! Did he just shoot and kill at least four people... one by one?

Cavius ended their drive at Sonic's Drive Thru that was close to the interstate. With her nerves gathered, Deja climbs into the front seat and stares at Cavius. He was now on his phone as if nothing ever happened. *How?*

"You want anything to eat?" Cavius asks Deja before placing the phone to his earlobe. She glares at him in utter disbelief.

"Hey, I'm going to need you to clear my schedule for the rest of the day," he calls and tells his secretary, and then hangs up. Cavius returns his attention back to Deja and asks her, "Do you know what you want to eat?"

"I don't want to eat nothing," Deja says in a low tone. "You just shot and killed them folks, Cavius!"

"Could you calm down. You're going to make me lose my appetite. Now I'm just going to order anything so it can look like we're not being idle. We need to talk right now," he then rolls down the window and presses the red circle button to make their order.

Deja deeply exhales as she found herself gathering her thoughts again. Deja couldn't come clean and tell him that she's been involved with some drug lord and his shady ass soldier that's now threatening to take her life and her kids in which she hadn't said nothing to anyone?! And then again, she has some questions for Cavius.

"You wanna go first or should I?" he asks Deja.

"Ladies before men," Deja shrugs her shoulders. "So

what the hell is you doing with a strap in your truck and where did you learn to shoot like that?"

"I always carry a gun with me, Deja. I do shit outside of work from time to time that requires me to move around carefully. I took shooting classes and all that. It is my right," he explains. "So… why did that car shoot at you that way?"

Deja swallows hard and fumbles with her nails, some she hasn't done in a while. "Um, honestly I don't know where to start. I keep trying to tell you that I'm bad. Not by my attitude or ways, but I'm used to getting money illegal ways. Whether it's selling drugs or robbing," she explains to him and then sighs.

"Tell me more, cause today you could've been dead. If you or your kids or all of y'all were in that lil house, y'all would not walk out to live and tell how someone sprayed it!" Cavius fusses at Deja.

"Some months ago, I helped my son out of the streets from selling dope before he got locked up. I missed the money and the thrill and I picked up my old ways again, selling it from time to time -"

"From who?" Cavius firmly asks with a tone in his voice, his elbow now propped on the armrest.

Deja sighs again and says, "From a guy named Trey." Cavius nods his head, but he didn't believe her.

"So what led to this shootout?"

Deja couldn't fix her mouth or words to tell him the truth, her eyes falling down to the floor.

"Okay, so you don't want to admit that you're so fucking bad enough to get in deep trouble! Fine, but I'm going to find out. I still have connections, Deja. My thing is, what will you do now that your house been sprayed?" he asks her.

They both glanced to see a nice girl come up to the

window carrying a red trey in her uniform and roller skates. With a smile on her face, she says, "Hey, here's your order! Your total is $12.59."

Deja watches as Cavius retrieves a twenty dollar bill from his wallet that rested in the cup holder and then gives it to the girl. "Keep the change, baby," he says to her. Deja frowns at his words.

"Thanks," she smiles, happily taking the money with her long, pink acrylic nails.

The girl give Cavius their food and then happily skates away. Deja watches him, puzzled by the way he went straight into eating.

"What's the matter with you?" Cavius then says after patting the sides of his mouth with a napkin.

"I'm disgusted," Deja bluntly says.

"So what are you going to do?" he asks her again, and then takes a manly bite out of his burger.

"I'm going to get that lil Jake nigga back!" Deja wanted to say but doesn't.

"I'll get a hotel room somewhere. It's nothing to me," Deja shrugs her shoulders.

"Tell you what. I have a lil family type of house out somewhere in the East off Hickory Hill. You and your girls can fall up in there until you can do better," he offers her.

"I don't need a hand-out or charity from you, Cavius! I'm a grown ass woman and I can handle myself!"

"Can you?"

"What the fuck you mean can I? Hell yeah I can!"

"Because from the looks of it, you're just another foolish woman out here making stupid ass decisions that's gonna cost either your kids' lives or yours!"

Deja couldn't hold her composure making Cavius catch a quick slap while he was taking a bite out of his burger. Startled by his calm reaction, she holds her breath and intensely watches him as he lowers his burger and places it down onto its wrapper. Cavius raises his hand and slaps Deja harder, busting her lips.

"Gr!" she growls in anger, getting out of her seat.

"Come on, baby!" Cavius taunts her. Deja climbs over and straddles Cavius, gripping his earlobes in her hands. He reaches up and grabs a handful of her hair, snatching it, making her head jerk back.

A server that's skating sees the scene and taps onto the window. "Mind your fucking business!" Deja loudly shouts from the window at the girl as Cavius leans forward and starts suckling her neck.

"I'm calling the police!" the girl yells back and rushes away.

Deja gives him a hard shove away from her and then opens the driver door, and calls at the girl, "What you say?" She crawls out the truck.

As she tried to shut the door, Cavius was coming after her, "Baby, come on and get back in the car. We'll leave. Let's leave!" Deja backs off, seeing the girl hurry into the restaurant. She and Cavius gets into the truck and he pulls out from the parking space.

The rest of the drive was silent until Cavius gets out his phone. Deja tunes into his conversation.

"Hey, Ivan. Yea, I need you to do a favor for me. I'm going to text you an address and the rest of some information," he gets straight to the point, and then hangs up.

"You're not gonna take me back?" Deja asks him.

"No, with me is where you and the girls need to be. You don't have to tell me the truth cause I'm going to find out either way," Cavius shrugs his shoulders.

Of all the men Deja have dated, she never seen them like Cavius before. He could handle her, but he's a man about things.

Picking the girls up from school, Deja swallows hard. Deja saw the question on their face when she pulled up with Cavius in his truck.

"Girls, I have something to tell you," she begin as they silently sat in the rear seat. "There was a house fire. I fell asleep and somehow the space heater caught on fire."

"Oh my god, mom. Are you okay?" Raine asks her. Cavius sighs as Deja nods her head.

"I'm fine, but I couldn't get everything," she starts to sob, because some of it was true. Although there wasn't a fire, Cavius wasn't having it with Deja going back to get her things!

"It's going to be okay mommy," Rylee says. Playing along, Cavius reaches over and soothingly massages Deja's shoulder with his free hand.

"So," she sniffles, gently wiping underneath her eyes. "Cavius here is going to let us sleep at his place until I can find us somewhere else." They remain quiet as Deja focuses her vision out the window. She can't believe today.

With one strap of her backpack on one shoulder, Raine stands around, not wanting to sit down or get comfortable just yet. She seen how her mom and sister easily settled into the nicely decorated living room while Cavius disappeared like a ghost. Raine walks over to the mantle of picture frames, showing Cavius with some other guys all in their suit and ties.

"Mom?" Raine calls from the other side of the room. "Maybe I don't know something of what I should," she later says.

"Meaning?" Deja inquires.

"What does this man do for a living again?" Raine turns to face her.

"He owns stock with Samsung and have his own business," Deja replies.

"Does it have a location? Have you seen it with your own two eyes?" Raine ponders.

"Yes."

"What kind of business?"

"Okay where is all of this coming from?" Deja snaps.

"This time around, mom, I ask the questions and you answer them!" Raine bad mouths her. Deja gets up from the couch and then walks over to Raine.

"Lil momma, I don't give a damn what go round it is! I'm the parent and you're the child. I don't have to answer shit you ask me! Period!" Deja looks Raine directly in the eyes.

"Winter break is next week. I'm going to dad's house," Raine says without breaking eye contact. Deja nods her head in agreement and then turns away from her.

After tucking Rylee into bed, Deja found Cavius in the living room, standing by the window that overlooked the river with a glass of brandy in his hand. "Hey?" she softly says, joining the side of him.

"Hey," he softly mumbles. "So you wanna talk to me about what happened earlier or you're still gonna let me find out for myself?"

Deja sighs and murmurs, "I'm going to need a drink."

She didn't feel like telling the truth, but Deja is alive because of him. They gathered on the two seat couch with their glasses of alcohol refilled in their hands.

Deja takes another sip of the smooth brown liquor and then clears her throat. "So, Trey had sent me and this kid named Jake out to do an exchange. It went wrong, and I seen Jake kill an innocent man which he told me to lie about. This can't get out to anyone cause he threatened to kill my boy in jail," Deja sighs, her eyes becoming glossy with tears.

"Why didn't you tell me this earlier? What was so hard about it?"

"Cause there's more to it! To ice the cake, he slapped me with his gun! I care about my babies but I can't protect Marterrio in jail. He's thinking I'll tell!" Deja holds her head in her hands, sniffling and tears falling down her cheeks. Setting down his glass, Cavius scoots closer to Deja and holds her in his arms as she sobs.

"I'll see what I can do to make sure he won't be touched while he's in there. Don't you worry about Jake anymore, okay?" he reassures Deja, speaking softly into her ear. Nodding her head, she holds onto him tighter.

It was no longer Deja's place to worry about what could happen to lil Jake. The following morning, Deja stuck to her usual routine by taking the girls to school after they got ready. Returning back, there was a white Volkswagen car parked near the walkway.

Getting out of the car, the first thing that Deja could hear is a man and woman arguing from nearby.

"I just want to know why, huh? Nigga I was there for you! Why is you doing me like this?" Taleah was yelling at Cavius with her hand on her hips as Deja now walks around the corner to see them, seeing that Taleah ain't so pregnant anymore.

"And on top of that, you bonded the bitch out of jail after what she did to me!" she says louder. Cavius' eyes goes from Taleah to Deja as he seen her near Taleah.

"I got your bitch right here, hoe!" Deja says, grabbing a handful of Taleah's expensive weave into her hands and then harshly yanking the woman back. Cavius hurries down from the porch to stop them. The two now had each other by the hair.

Deja takes her hand and quickly tightens it into a fist

122

and connects her knuckles to Taleah's head saying, "Let my hair go bitch! Let my hair go!"

"Damn, Deja! Don't do this here!" Cavius firmly says. Releasing Taleah, Deja harshly shoves the short woman.

"I will not be disrespected from anyone! Baby mommas included," Deja firmly says, her eyes directly on Taleah as she combs out her weave with her short, sausage fingers.

"You gone regret that, believe me!"

"I don't give a fuck about what you got to say! I won't take any disrespect!" Deja pounds her fist into her hand as she talks.

"You need to be going," Cavius orders Taleah.

"And what about the baby, Cavius?" Taleah whines, her voice breaking.

"You're not trying to let things blow over and give me time neither! Look at how you're acting. I'm trying to start some new with Deja and you just being psychotic! I'll wait to see my child. Bye!" Cavius waves his hand at Taleah. She scoffs and flips her hair, brushing her shoulder against Deja as she struts away.

Deja walks up to Cavius and jokes with him, "What I tell you about entertaining goblins?" Cavius tries not to laugh, deeply sighing and turning away on his heels. The two of them went inside the condo, settling into the kitchen. As they enter, she spots a folded wad of cash on the counter.

"So, I've been thinking about you and I have a job for you," Cavius says.

Deja's mouth nearly drops, as she says, "A job for me? Like a real job where I'm getting paid?"

"Some like that. Sort of like a real job where you'll be getting paid and calling all the shots. What you'll make in a day will be more than your normal paycheck. Or you can let me take care of you?"

Leaning onto the counter with the money atop it, Deja grins to herself, indecisive and unclear of what she wanted to do.

"In the meantime, why don't you go and treat yourself. Get a massage. Hook up with your coworker for brunch. You deserve it, Deja. You deserve some *me* time," he says.

"I can't take this, Cavius. I don't know where it came from," she sighs. Deja didn't know what the hell she was saying. Cavius offering her a lot of money was all too unreal. "I mean how much is this?"

"I'm hoping it's enough to make you feel good about yourself again. I don't want you to worry and I mean that, Deja. I have to start getting ready to leave for work," Cavius exits the kitchen without another word. Deja's eyes trails down to the thick wad of cash. She has no clue of how she's going to spend it.

Chapter 8

Standing across from each other, Deja takes a long pull from her cigarette and then exhales its smoke from her nostrils. "Been thinking about you and what happened. Why you went ghost?"

"Ask Lil Jake, he knows why," she replies to him.

"I ain't gone lie. I haven't heard from lil nigga in almost a week now," Cane says with suspicion in his tone.

"Well, I'm out... For real this time," Deja firmly says.

"If you say so," Cane chuckles in his throat and then walks away.

Wearing her new favorite pair of expensive heels with a Fendi poncho over a black turtleneck shirt, Deja happily struts away. She'd do anything for Cavius. If he wanted her to hide his gun, she'd do it! If Cavius tells her to stop having contact with drug lords and her clients?,Deja would get rid of her old phone and get a new one with a new email address to sync with it, which she did.

Although Raine was going through her phases and different moods and attitudes, Deja could make her daughters happy without worrying herself with how she'll pay

125

the next bill. On weekends, Deja and the girls went out more with Cavius. He's real good with getting through to her kids unlike Deja's ex. Cavius showed Deja an unseen Memphis and he never involved her into his other business.

Picking up the girls from school, Deja was trying to figure out why Raine's friend was happily trailing after her towards the car. After letting Rylee get in first, Raine climbs in next with her friend, Venus behind them.

"Hey, Miss Deja," she says with a large smile. Raine had to go and make friends with the only White girl in a predominately Black school. Deja wasn't surprised because her dad is biracial and enjoys the company of both races, White and Black.

"Hello, Venus. Why your uncle didn't pick you up?" Deja asks, not sugar coating anything. She has shopping plans with the girls right after school to get them ready to send them down to Georgia.

"Mom, really?" Raine says with an attitude.

"Really, really," Deja murmurs, shifting the gear stick into drive.

"It's totally fine," Venus says. "You should tell your mom though, Raine."

"Tell me what?"

"She's coming with us to Georgia," Raine happily says. "I already asked dad and Cavius and it's fine with them both, so you're out-ruled on this mom." Deja remains calm, taking a deep breath as the two of them were giggling and snickering like the two teenage girls they were.

"My mom's friend giving us some shopping money too!" Raine happily says and they giggle together.

Deja couldn't wait to get rid of the girls that evening. It gave her enough energy to be all over Cavius with him inside her. With no more walls up, letting Cavius inside, they had finally connected on a level like never before...

more than just sexually but spiritually. Deja has never got to know a man before that was good for the soul the way Cavius is.

The following morning, Cavius had left Deja sleeping in the bed late. The heavy drapes were drawn over the windows blocking out the sun rays as the hard rain from outside drummed against the roof and windows.

Peeping with one eye open, Deja seen how Cavius wasn't in bed and the time was past ten in the morning. After climbing out of bed, Deja went right into the bathroom to handle her hygiene. She then slips into her new, lavender satin robe with matching fur slippers and exits the bathroom.

It's eleven in the afternoon and she's still hungry for some more of Cavius. Deja happily struts from the hallway and through the kitchen, her pussy was hot and throbbing. "Oh, Cavius?" Deja sings, seeing that he had already cooked breakfast and eaten.

"I hoped you saved room for dessert, daddy," she says, entering into the living room to see two of him sitting on the couch. Deja abruptly stops and folds her arms across her breasts. Unable to tell the two apart, she says, "What the hell is this?"

"Good afternoon," his identical brother says with a softer tone than Cavius. He was the same height as Cavius, too, but with lesser muscles.

"Deja," Cavius raises from the couch and then walks over to her. "This is one of my brothers I been trying to get you to meet," Cavius introduces him.

"I'm Cooper," he says, still sitting down on the couch with a nice smile. "We're missing one which is Caleb but he likes to be called Cane," he later adds. Deja's soul wanted to leave her body and float away. She did her best to hide the shocked expression on her face.

127

"Why would he want to be called a name other than his own?"

"He got locked up by the feds one time before. Aliases are better than street nicknames," Cavius explains and then takes Deja by the hand and pulls her to the side.

She didn't give him a chance to talk. Fuming right away, "Wow, Cavius! At least wake me up and let me know what's going on!"

"I know, but you look so damn beautiful when you're asleep. Why don't you go and slip into something warm? We're going to have brunch with my brothers in another hour," Cavius informs her. Deja gently sighs.

"Both of them?" Deja asks. *But why?*

"Yes, both of them. It's a private celebration for each of us, starting with me. I just sealed a two million dollar deal on a foundation engaging and encouraging men of all ages and walks of life to be great," he smiles from ear to ear.

"Then you don't think something like this calls for a dinner rather than brunch?" Deja suggests with a smile.

"You could be right but we all agreed on brunch. It's the least part of the day that doesn't have us busy like the night does. Go on and get dressed," Cavius then walks away.

Deja pulls on a long sleeve, red wine colored sweater dress with black tights underneath, and a pair of flat knee boots. She curls and styles her long hair, later putting on her simple jewelry that didn't cost much to her.

Even though Deja had some sort of interaction with Cane, gazing at her reflection, she's still happy with the woman she is with Cavius. Her mind is in a better space. He doesn't destroy her peace. He makes her feel like a woman and more.

"You look so damn beautiful," Cavius' voice says from

across the room as Deja was now placing on her black, motorcycle jacket. She smiles and struts over to him; they gently kiss each other on the lips.

"Thanks," she says. "I'm still not your height."

"What fun it is in that. Let's go," Cavius takes Deja by the hand.

Deja was a nervous wreck, sitting at the table with just Cavius and Cooper with his girlfriend. She hid her hands under the table in her lap to fumble with her fingers, and she nibbles on the tastebuds of her tongue.

Cavius beams over at Deja, noticing how silent she's been. After gently clearing his throat, Cavius leans in closer to Deja and asks, "Are you alright?"

"No, I'm about to shit a brick right in this chair!" Deja wanted to reply. She looks at him and answers, "Yea I need to go to the restroom."

"Sure, what will you have to drink when the server comes back?" Cavius reaches over and holds her hand in his as Deja raises up from her chair.

"Just get me whatever you're drinking on," Deja softly says to him and then walks away. She couldn't wait to make it to the hallway, finding herself nearly running to the women's restroom.

Hiding in the stall, Deja pulls herself together. Every lie to tell ran through her mind. She had never been caught up until now.

"Breathe, bitch," Deja gently exhales. "Just breathe. You got this." After pep-talking herself, Deja exits the stall, encountering a beautiful, tall, dark-skinned woman with long flowing hair down to her waist line in the mirror.

"Heard you in there pep-talking yourself," the woman grins with a smile, taking a red tube of lipstick across her full lips.

Excuse me, bitch? Deja was startled by her height; she was no longer sure if the woman was in the right restroom.

"It's okay," she smiles at her reflection. "I do it all the time when I know I'm about to be in the same room with two different men I have affections for," she flips her long hair and then struts out of the restroom. Deja sighs and follows behind her, leading both of their short walk right to the same table.

Cane had now joined them at the table. The tall beauty from the ladies room takes a chair on the side of him. Grinning, she leans in to kiss him on the cheek, leaving a stain of her red lipstick on his flesh. Cane blushes and she playfully wipes his cheek clean as Deja takes her seat on the side of Cavius.

"Oh, you're back. This is our brother and his fiancé, Caleb and Zhara," Cooper introduces them.

Caleb and Zhara, huh? Ain't this about a bitch! Fiancé?! With her drink on the table, Deja plays off her jealousy and acts casual. "She's beautiful," Deja comments the woman. "You two make a great couple."

"You know it's real when he gives you the ring in less than three months," Zhara jokes, she and Caleb sharing a laugh together. Deja suckles her teeth and then takes a sip from her cocktail drink. *You don't say.*

The more they sat around and ate and gossiped or talked, the more Deja got comfortable with seeing *Caleb* with his fiancé. It was like she hadn't become familiar with him at all except for on today.

Feeling safe and secure, Deja walks on the side of Cavius with their arms hooked around each other as they all exit the restaurant. "That was so refreshing," Cooper's sweet girlfriend Rita says. She wasn't a low-key alley cat like Deja and Zhara. Rita's a graduate of the University of

Memphis with her Bachelor's Degree in Psychology and a part of Alpha Kappa Alpha.

"Wasn't it though? You all should try this place off of Park with us some day," Zhara suggests, four inches taller than Cane. Deja still couldn't believe that he has a whole fiancé that's been hiding with a tree somewhere!

Reaching their car, Cavius turns to face Deja and they briefly kiss each other. "I hope you saved room for dessert," Deja flirts with him, pulling Cavius closer by the collar of his trench coat.

"Always," he grins from ear to ear, leaning in to kiss her again.

Cavius then reaches down and opens the car door for Deja. Lowering herself down into Cavius's brand new, Ferrari, Deja catches a glimpse of Cane glaring her way. He then quickly looks away before Zhara could catch him. Deja grins to herself as Cavius shuts the door and then walks over to the driver's side.

"Take your tights off," Cavius orders Deja after he cranks up the car. Obedient, Deja lifts her body upward and removes her tights from her cold legs.

After waiting for the car to heat up, Cavius reaches over and takes his hand underneath Deja's dress tail. Ready as she was, Deja props her right foot onto the dashboard and sets her seat back, getting more pleasure as Cavius gently massages and caresses her clitoris with his forefinger tip.

Deja moans in ecstasy and grips onto the seatbelt as Cavius' finger stirs around her pussy juices, going at a medium speed and then real slow. With one hand on the steering wheel and the other playing in Deja's wet pussy, Cavius' eyes glares down at his cell phone now ringing in the cup holder. He was hoping that it'd stop ringing, but Cane was calling again.

Removing his hand, Deja takes it and then inserts the same finger he used on her, into her mouth, tasting herself with her eyes close. Cavius was going to answer the phone until he felt the growing hardness in his pants. Right when he reached the interstate, Cavius pulls over to the curb and unbuttons his pants, whipping out his long rod.

Deja wanted to taste it, but instead, Cavius says, "Turn around."

"Okay," Deja says.

She was expecting him to go soft and for his strokes to be rhythmic like always, but Cavius's body was heavy on her and he was rough. Deja's knees buckled and she held on tight to the armrest of the seat as Cavius pounds himself in and out of her; obviously her pussy liked it from the way it was wet and ready.

"Aahhh!" Cavius says, coming inside Deja as he went deep, the tip of his dick touching her cervix sending chills through her body.

As he pulls away, Deja finally glances up to see there's a police squad car parked right behind them.

"Shit!" she hisses, tugging at Cavius's shirt. "Baby look!" Deja then points past the rear windshield.

Cavius sees the driver's door opening on the squad car, the officer leg sticking out from the bottom and says, "Just hold on tight."

"Hold on tight?" Deja softly quotes after him, her brows pressed together.

With his clothes fixed again, Cavius changes the gear shift and then speeds off, his right foot mashing the gas pedal. Deja's head jerks back into the headrest and she grips onto the side of the door. Her eyes go over to the dashboard, seeing the speedometer increase up to a hundred miles.

Cavius jumped and switched from lane to lane, driving

fast like a crazed driver until he thought the police was no longer going to find him. Deja didn't release the side of the door until they reached the city speed limit.

Sighing, Cavius says, "You are kind of nonchalant in a blunt way."

Taking his words into offense, Deja flips her hair and says, "Well, Cavius! I'm not used to lying to a law enforcement officer."

"How do you steal shit, but can't lie?" he briefly looks over at Deja and then returns his eyes back to the road.

"Used to, nigga! I used to steal things and that's different. It doesn't take much thinking to go and steal something," she deeply exhales. *But it does; it takes a lot of thinking to put together how you're going to steal whatever you had plans to.*

"So how sticky are your fingers?" Cavius asks her.

"Not sticky at all," Deja looks out the window. "I don't walk into stores or people houses and clip them, Cavius. I wait until you or your shit is vulnerable for the taking." She flips her hair again and then waves her hand in midair in dismissal.

With Cavius having a business agenda, he drops Deja off and then leaves her with an extra five thousand dollars and access to his other vehicles. Bored and alone with the hired maid from a cleaning service tidying up the condo, Deja gets her phone and dials Melissa's number.

"Hello?" Melissa's jolly voice answers the phone. Deja could hear a lot of excitement and noise going on in the background.

"Hey, are you busy?" Deja asks Melissa.

"Nope, you just hear my husband's friends and him in the background. Wanna come over?"

"I was thinking we'd talk over the phone," Deja advises and then nervously chuckles at the long pause of silence from Melissa's end. "But I have nothing else better to do," Deja later says.

"Okay great. No, it's fine. We can talk. I'm making the guys some more of those ham and cheese sliders anyways," Melissa chuckles as Deja exhales in relief.

Ham and cheese sliders… what the fuck? Melissa has the lifestyle that Deja wanted but not the type of marriage. She's in her middle thirties now with a five-year-old and still unmarried. Deja couldn't see herself making finger food for her husband's guests that'll crowd the living room with their loud voices, shouting and rooting for their teams during football season. She's comfortable with the way things are with Cavius… uncommitted.

"Okay cool, so you know this mountain of mine has an identical twin brother and another one," Deja starts, prancing her way into the kitchen. She was up for a glass of Cavius's expensive white wine.

"Really? But you said he had siblings though," her tone was obvious.

"Yea, but the gag is, before we got serious and moved in together, I was being a thot and kind of probably toyed around with the other brother," Deja admits to Melissa and then glances over her shoulder to see if the maid was eavesdropping.

"What?" Melissa sings and then giggles. Deja sighs in relief and then pores the wine into the glass. "There's no judgement here honey bee. You're in a none committed relationship and unmarried to him. So, what's the problem?"

"There isn't one. It's just that we all went to brunch and the brother had a girl with him, too, so I guess there's no foul or harm in that. I just never been in such a situation before," Deja walks away from the counter with her glass in her hand.

"Well as long as your feelings aren't caught up between two brothers, you should be fine, Deja."

"You're right but what if the other brother go and tells Cavius about us?"

"Were y'all ever intimate?"

"We probably might've kissed a time or two, but I don't know how his brother feels about me."

"Honey there's only one way to find out. If Cane starts to get down into his brother's ear canal about you two and have malicious lies instead of telling the truth, then there's a chance of your word being against his could save your relationship or not, depending if Cavius is a sucker for you," Melissa says. "Hey hold on... Henry?! What the hell are these?" she yells at someone over the phone.

"My son Henry just loves being a nature expert. He takes dirt and tries to grow things with it in my damn Tupperware bowls!" Melissa fumes over the phone, the sounds of cabinet doors being slammed shut in the background.

"So who did you meet first, huh?" Melissa asks Deja, her voice more calm.

"I met the brother first but it wasn't on some romantic type of shit though," Deja sets her glass down onto the elegant iron and glass end table and then flops down onto the couch.

Beep, beep!

A breakthrough call alerts Deja. She pulls the phone away from her ear right as Melissa starts to talk, seeing that it's an unfamiliar number calling. "Hey, what'd you say again?" Deja asks Melissa.

"Well you're going to be fine, Deja. Stop worrying yourself so much," Melissa happily says.

Maybe Melissa is right, but she doesn't have a clue of the type of man Cane is... he has more street in him than

135

Cavius. He didn't forget where he come from. Cane has that rough edge in him that drives a woman wild. Cane has the streets and guns but Cavius has the power and money.

After talking with Melissa over the phone, Deja found herself something to get into. She didn't call the nail shop to schedule an appointment or make reservations at some restaurant. In the back of her mind, Deja knew that her relationship with Cavius wouldn't be *forever*.

She searched the internet until she ran across an idea of what business she should start. With her polished nails, Deja brainstorms on ideas until her cell phone loudly rang on the desk. She glances over at the phone, seeing that it's the same unfamiliar number from earlier.

A chilling feeling creeps up Deja's spine as she reaches over to pick up the phone. Quickly swiping her finger across the screen, answering it, Deja then taps the speaker icon and says, "Hello?"

"So," his voice says in a low tone. After suckling his teeth, Cane says, "So, you're fucking my brother huh?"

"I'm dating him, yea," Deja confirms. Cane suckles his teeth again on the other end of the phone and then exhales.

Deja takes the phone off the speaker and says, "Don't you have a whole fiancé Mister Big Stuff?"

"That ain't got shit to do with you fucking my brother, bitch!" he shouts at her. "Zhara is different. She's a bitch that my brothers never dealt with before!"

"You think so?" Deja challenges him. "Why are you blowing up about what me and your brother have going on, Caleb?"

"Don't nobody ever calls me by my fucking government name! I wanna know so I can start knowing how to deal with you!" Cane blows up. Deja briefly moves the phone away from her earlobe, and then puts it back.

"Just know I choose him, Cane. I wasn't supposed to have as many close calls with you the way that I had. And I love your brother. He's made me a better woman. You should be more focused on your engagement," Deja calmly says.

"I never knew you to be the type to be a gold digging ass bitch!" he bad mouths her.

Deja cackles and says in protest, "You never knew me enough at all, Cane. And your brother's a better man than you!"

"You wanna bet bitch! You wanna go gambling with his life in your hands, huh?"

"No, I don't want to go doing none of that! It's just facts, Cane."

"Hear ye, hear ye, bitch! Who do you choose, me or him?" the tone of Cane's voice is hostile and brute. Deja could tell he wasn't too pleased about his engagement to Zhara and her relationship with Cavius.

"You're a greedy motherfucker, Cane! You know that right?"

"Me or him, Deja?"

"Cavius," she says, shortly hearing the ending dial of the tone. He had hung up in her face. Deja sets down her phone onto the smooth surface of the desk and then reclines back into the chair, deep in her thoughts of what's to come next.

Deja was fine until the night came when Cavius didn't return home. She didn't want to pester him with phone calls, helping herself to another cup of wine after the next until his number pops up on her phone's screen.

"Hello?"

"Hey, I see you're still up," his voice calmly says, soothing her mind. But then Cavius is mysterious at times; a man with silent emotions.

"Yea, I've been here all day," Deja sighs.

"I'm sorry babe. I been out taking care of business and stuff," he explains. "I'm bringing in take out on my way in; is that fine?"

"You know what? I can order take out from one of these surrounding restaurants," Deja suggests.

"Okay, that's cool. I'll see you in a little while then."

"Okay," Deja smiles to herself and they both end their phone call. With her mind at rest, Deja was now able to relax, fixing herself another cup of wine and soaking her body into a hot tub of water.

With her hair pinned up into a messy bun and her back pressed against the soft, cushioned pillow, Deja slumps down further into the tub and closes her eyes. Her thoughts drifts to how good life is, a life that Deja never knew she was capable of having. She'd do anything to keep her relationship with Cavius and her position on lockdown.

Drowsy and in deep relaxation, Deja dozes off, nearly submitting the rest of her torso deeper into the water. Resting, Deja gently moans at the feel of someone's hands massaging her shoulders.

"Feels good," she softly murmurs to Cavius. "I love it when you're caring like this."

Seeing how he didn't respond, Deja wakes up and her eyes trail down at the soft, feminine dark skin hands on her shoulders. Before she could scream or react, the female has forced Deja down into the water and pins her down.

It burns her eye to see through the water, frowning to see Zhara with an evil grin on her face! Deja thought she was dreaming until she starts losing oxygen.

Reaching out the water, Deja tried to grab for Zhara's face which she moves away, stretching her neck from side to side. Deja would've grabbed her hair if she didn't have it pinned away. Kicking and reaching, and running out of air to breathe, Deja then grabs her shirt collar. With a tight grip, she pulls Zhara down towards her, quickly reaching around with her other hand and snatches Zhara's studded earring from her ear hole.

"Ah!" Zhara screams and releases Deja, quickly scurrying away. Deja pulls herself through the water, gasping for air and gathering her head. Now pissed off and filled with rage, Deja climbs out of the tub and retrieves her bathrobe, tipping out the bathroom.

Deja moves quickly, running right into Cavius's closet for his gun, something she ran across while going through his things. She checks it, making sure that the safety pin was off and it had bullets in the chamber; Deja only needed one!

"Zhara? Come out wherever you are, bitch?" Deja loudly taunts her, carefully tipping down the hallway.

Hearing a noise in the kitchen, Deja hastily turns the corner and openly fires, hitting the wall. Spotting Zhara quickly run past the doorway that lead to the living room, Deja pursues after her.

She chases her, following after Zhara into the garage where Deja fires again. Zhara screams and hits the smooth, cement floor. Tightly gripping the gun in her hand, Deja approaches Zhara on the ground, scared and afraid. Deja's always been against guns until the recent occur of events.

"Why you here, bitch?" Deja asks her.

"Cause you think you're the only one that used to love two brothers, huh? Do you think it's fair to have Cane compete with Cavius for your love?" she asks Deja in response.

"You're a special kind of stupid to answer me with some questions! I choose Cavius; that's who I love. I never wanted any competition between them!"

"Tell it to Cane," Zhara smiles from ear to ear.

Deja grimaces and lifts the gun in the air and says, "You crazy bitch!"

At the alarming sound of footsteps, Deja turns around in enough time to see five police officers fill the garage. With their guns aiming at her, one of them yells, "Put the weapon down now!"

"Help! Thank goodness you've arrived!" Zhara cries out from behind Deja. Deja moves slowly, obediently placing the gun down onto the cement floor.

"Turn around with your hands over your head now!" the same officer orders her. Silent and crying, Deja turns around on her heels, glaring down at Zhara with a smirk across her face. Hot and angry tears streams down Deja's cheeks as they quickly placed a pair of cold handcuffs around her wrists. She jerks as they clutches down hard onto them. As they read Deja her Miranda rights, they escorted her out the garage door that leads to the back-street where their vehicles were parked.

She spots Cane talking to one of them and then loudly asks the officer, "Is she alright?"

"Yea, thanks for calling us. We got here in enough time," the officer says. Glancing her way, Cane grins at Deja before rushing away. The officer lowers her down into the police car, gently shoving her head down. Deja angrily watches with angry tears in her eyes that refuse to fall as Cane runs into the garage where she had just shot Zhara at, the other police officers surrounding each other.

"Deja Allen!" the bailiff now loudly calls, nearly startling Deja as she had dozed off to sleep on the bench of the uncomfortable holding cell.

She stands up and walks over to the cell door. Deja was so happy to be walked to the outside, Cavius waited inside his warm car with the heat on medium, grimly gazing at

Deja as she walks over to the car. Before she can pull on the handle, Deja hears the door locks.

She tugs on the handle still seeing that it's locked. Deja frowns and then bends over low enough to glance at Cavius through the dark, factory tint of the window. As he cracks the window open at the top, Deja says, "Is you serious?"

"You took the words right out my mouth," he calmly says.

"Cavius, unlock the door," she demands.

"I'm just sitting here debating should I leave your ass here to find your own ride back or not," he glares at her. Cavius seen how the emotion in Deja's face shifted to sadness. "Oh, you didn't think I'd let you off that easy huh?"

Deja shakes her head from side to side and says, "What were you told?"

"I just want to know were you aware that me and this nigga was brothers before you decided to keep going back and biting into the forbidden, rotten fruit?" Cavius asks her.

"No." Deja's eyes fills with tears, seeing Cavius glance away in disdain like he didn't believe her. "I swear to you, Cavius! I didn't know until we went to brunch." Without saying get in, Cavius unlocks the doors. Deja hurries into the car and places her hands over the vent of the car to warm them up.

Their whole ride back to the condo was silent between them with no words to be exchanged. Pulling underneath the garage, Deja notices a small stain in the cement where Zhara had fell when she shot her. She deeply sighs and then glares over at Cavius. The two of them didn't bother getting out of the vehicle at once, leaving the car running.

Deja remains calm and then reaches over to hug him,

but Cavius stops her arms and deeply sighs. "You want me to go? Want me to leave?" Deja asks him, her voice breaking.

"That's not what I said. I just don't know. I've invested my heart, money, and time into this relationship with you. I want to know is you down for me?" Cavius gleams at Deja.

"Of course -"

"Because it's either us or him. Let me show you something," Cavius reaches over and pulls down the door of the glove compartment, pulling a gun from it. He tosses the heavy piece of steel into Deja's lap and then sits back into his seat.

Cavius glares at Deja, observant and watching for her reaction. With her eyes fixed down at the gun, Deja then returns her gaze to Cavius. "What are you…" she couldn't find the words to say anymore. Deja swallows hard, breaking eye contact from Cavius.

"You say you're down for me, then get rid of Cane. Or else leave me the hell alone, cause let me tell you something, Deja. I've already been through this before with Cane and I let him win with Zhara. Now here we go again and I'm just not up for any bargains or deals this time around."

"You just put a gun in my lap. What you want me to do?"

"I already told you. Get rid of him, Deja."

"You want me to kill him?!"

Cavius raises his brows and then sighs. "Or you can just walk away with your kids and money while you can. Only you have a point to prove here."

"I don't have not one motherfucking point to prove to nobody!" Deja sasses him. Cavius quickly reaches over and then grabs the back of Deja's neck.

"Damnit, Deja! I fucking love you! Either choose me or

end up in a pine box at the bottom of the river!" Cavius threatens Deja, ringing onto her neck like a chicken, then later releasing her. Deja was shocked and afraid at the same time.

Catching his breath, Cavius asks her, "Is you going to do it?"

Deja repeatedly nods her head and says, "Yes, but I don't want to go to jail."

"You're not; just trust in me," Cavius finally turns off the car and exits, leaving Deja by herself with the gun.

For Christmas, Cavius had rented a house in Arlington for the majority of their family to come over and eat. The girls wanted to spend Christmas Day with their dad, leaving Deja alone with all her woes. Mesmerized at her stunning reflection in the mirror, Deja takes her hand and picks up her glass of cranberry with vodka. She sips away her fears for the evening and then picks up the small hunting knife from off the vanity counter.

After there was a gentle tap on the door, Deja watches in the mirror to see Cavius enter with his matching suit to hers. She continues to tuck the knife down between her breasts, securing it just between the fat meat of her breasts and corset. Approaching Deja, Cavius rests his hands on her bare shoulders and then leans down to inhale her sweet perfume. "You look amazing," he whispers into her ear.

Deja grins and says, "It's all for you, baby."

"Let's get going," he says.

Hand in hand, Cavius and Deja walks from the bedroom and to the dinner room where everyone was at, adults and children present. Everyone was looking gracious and elegant in their Christmas outfits. Cavius introduced Deja to almost everyone attending until they stumbled across Cane.

He had a sinister and mysterious gleam in his eyes,

coming alone. Cane suckles his teeth and says, "Well, well, what do we have here?"

"Good evening," Cavius grins at him.

"Ain't no fucking good evening, motherfucker!" Cane spats at him.

"Where's Zhara?" Deja asks him.

"Bitch, why don't you ask your man?" Cane snaps at her.

"Excuse me, who you calling a bitch? Bitch!"

Cavius pulls Deja behind him and stands between she and Cane, who steps up to him. The three of them glance around seeing if anyone was paying attention to them, pulling themselves together.

"So, where is Zhara?" Deja turns to ask Cavius.

"I don't know," he answers.

"*Tsk!*" Cane loudly suckles his teeth and shakes his head from side to side. Cavius takes Deja by the hand and then guides her away, leading her to the front of the room.

"Can I get everyone's attention, please!" he loudly says. Deja nervously stands on the side of Cavius, now feeling as though the knife between her breasts and dress was taking up oxygen all on its own. Deja couldn't believe she found herself in this kind of predicament.

Cane didn't deserve her love, but neither did he deserve for his life to be in her hands. Peering at Cavius, Deja now thought of him as a different man from the one she went to bed with the other night? Maybe Cavius is playing some sick joke on her and Cane with the help of Cooper? She wished that none of this is real.

"Ladies and gentlemen, strong and beautiful, it doesn't take much to describe the essence of this woman that has entered my life. I thought I'd never meet a woman like my mother until I met you, Deja," Cavius directs his words at Deja with a grin on his face, turning to face her.

"Cavius?" Deja asks in a low tone and then swallows hard, her heart beating fast. Watching Cavius dig into his pocket and quickly getting down onto one knee, Deja held her breath. *Boy, you better get up!* Deja steals a quick glance at the watching crowd of family members before returning her gaze down to Cavius.

He opens a small, square shaped box with a princess cut, 14 karat yellow diamond encrusted into a sterling silver ring. "Will you marry me?" Cavius asks her. Deja now felt light headed, wobbling towards Cavius and pressing her hands onto his shoulders to hold her weight.

Cavius sees the faint look over her face and then stands up. "Think of your future and your children, Deja?" he says, low enough for the two of them to only hear.

She was shaking her head in agreement when the crowd claps their hands and cheers for them. Cavius slides the ring onto Deja's finger and then kisses her by surprise. After pulling away from Cavius, Deja searches the crowd for Cane, seeing him passing through every-one. Cavius grins from ear to ear watching Deja leave him; he knew why. He sighs as she disappears behind the door.

He lingers behind as she chases after Cane. "Caleb?!" Deja calls after him once she catches up to him. Cane quickly turns around and then cuffs his big hands over Deja's neck, lifting her into the air, her feet dangling.

Cane had his hands tightly clutched around Deja's neck that she couldn't scream. Seeing her eyes turning red and her face a different color, Cane releases Deja. She fell to the ground, rolling up to sit and catch her breath. Cane grunts and continues walking away, saying, "Don't come after me again!"

"C-C-Cane...p-p-please!" Deja says between breath-ing, stretching her arms out to him. "Tell me what happened?" she had forced herself to holler at him, now choking and still gasping for air.

Quickly spinning around on his heels, Cane marches up to Deja and says, "One day I seen Zhara, and then the next day I didn't! I guess he took her out before he made your bail. Just stay away from me, aight?"

"Both of you motherfuckers are crazy!" Deja thinks to herself, seeing him angrily walk away.

A minute later, Cavius emerges from the house. Deja refuses his help and gets off the ground by herself. She frowns at Cavius, and says with tears in her eyes, "Did you do all that for show? That's your way of killing him?"

"You really thought that I meant murdering him? You're really that bad," Cavius says. Deja angrily lifts her hand and slaps him hard, making Cavius head turn into a different direction.

"You're sick!" Deja cries, her voice breaking; they make eye contact again. Cavius reaches out to touch the side of Deja's face until she slaps his hand away. Angry and biting her lip, Deja shakes her head from side to side.

"Just go," Cavius shrugs his shoulders, sadness filling his face. Turning on his heels, Cavius starts to walk away until there was the alarming sound of gunshots from behind him. Before he could duck, the firing stops followed by tires screeching the pavement, leaving Cavius in suspense until he turns and catches Deja.

He looks up to see Cane speeding down the street before returning his attention back to Deja. Cavius gently lowered them both to the cold ground, her warm blood quickly seeping through the material of her dress.

Subscribe

Text Shan to 22828 to stay up to date with new releases, sneak peeks, contest, and more....